One thing was missing.

"Hey, you." As if he'd heard her thoughts, Josh appeared.

"I thought you'd ditched me."

"Not hardly," he drawled with a lazy grin. "Been arranging a horse for your niece."

Heather smiled. "How do you always have a solution to my problems?"

"A knack for being in the right place at the right time, I guess."

And for stepping up to do more than any girl had a right to expect, she thought.

That's when she realized she could be in trouble with this country boy. She'd always been too independent to lean on someone, too afraid they'd leave.

Would Josh?

"That's a serious face," he teased, ticking her nose. "What's going on in that pretty head?"

"Just thinking. You know, guys usually tell me I'm too much work. Why don't you feel that way?"

She held her breath to hear his reply.

"Some things are worth the effort. And—" he pulled down his hat in a rakish pose "—there's nothing I like more than a good challenge."

Mia Ross loves great stories. She enjoys reading about fascinating people, long-ago times and exotic places. But only for a little while, because her reality is pretty sweet. Married to her college sweetheart, she's the proud mom of two amazing kids, whose schedules keep her hopping. Busy as she is, she can't imagine trading her life for anyone else's—and she has a pretty good imagination. You can visit her online at miaross.com.

Books by Mia Ross

Love Inspired

Oaks Crossing

Her Small-Town Cowboy
Rescued by the Farmer
Hometown Holiday Reunion
Falling for the Single Mom

Barrett's Mill

Blue Ridge Reunion
Sugar Plum Season
Finding His Way Home
Loving the Country Boy

Holiday Harbor

Rocky Coast Romance
Jingle Bell Romance
Seaside Romance

Visit the Author Profile page
at Harlequin.com for more titles.

Falling for the Single Mom

Mia Ross

HARLEQUIN® LOVE INSPIRED®

Recycling programs
for this product may
not exist in your area.

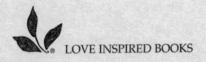 LOVE INSPIRED BOOKS

ISBN-13: 978-0-373-89912-8

Falling for the Single Mom

www.Harlequin.com

Printed in U.S.A.

We live by believing, not by seeing.
—*2 Corinthians* 5:7

For all the kind, compassionate people
who care for the animals we love.

Acknowledgments

Grateful to the very talented folks who help me
make my books everything they can be:
Melissa Endlich, Giselle Regus and
the dedicated staff at Love Inspired.

More thanks to the gang at Seekerville,
www.seekerville.net, a great place to
hang out with readers—and writers.

I've been blessed with a wonderful network of
supportive, encouraging family and friends.
You inspire me every day!

Chapter One

This was not happening.

Unclenching her teeth, Heather Fitzgerald called up the sweet smile that had gotten her out of so many scrapes in the past. "But you don't understand. All this—" she motioned at the large moving truck "—wasn't supposed to be here until Wednesday. This is Monday."

"Lady, you're the one who don't understand," the driver retorted in a manner that clearly announced he couldn't have cared any less. "I start in Cincy, then make a loop around four different states before I head back home. Sometimes it takes me a week, sometimes more'n that. This time, it took less, and I'm here now. If you want your load delivered later, I should be coming through here again in two or three weeks. But it'll cost you to store this stuff at our facility till then, and I can't make you any promises about when it'll actually show up."

After four years in college and four more slaving away day and night to get her veterinary degree, Heather had become adept at scheduling her life to the nth degree and keeping everything on track. It was midway through April, and the past few months had wreaked havoc with her normally precise planning. Somehow, using grit and bullish determination, she'd managed to squeak through with her sanity intact. Most of it, anyway.

So, because she was desperate, she decided it was time to try a different tactic. While she was far from the helpless female he obviously assumed her to be, she figured it couldn't hurt to appeal to his male pride. Pulling out her phone, she called up her ace in the hole.

"I hate to be a pest about this, but I really can't let these things be shuttled off to who-knows-where. My niece—" she showed him a picture of five-year-old Bailey "—has been living out of her suitcase since we arrived in town this past weekend. She became an orphan recently, and it's very important that she feels at home here as soon as possible."

"I've heard every story in the book," he grumbled, but he gave the screen a cursory glance before frowning. "I think you're yanking my chain about her being your niece. She looks just like you."

"Of course she does," Heather snapped, dangerously close to being out of patience. "Her father was my brother."

She could tell by the softening of his features that he was beginning to waver. Rubbing his neck, he said, "I'd like to help you, but I got other people's things on here, too, y'know."

"Come on, man" came a mellow drawl from behind her. "Give the lady a break."

Turning, she found herself nose-to-chest with a dark green T-shirt sporting an embroidered running horse over script that read Gallimore Stables—Oaks Crossing, Kentucky. As her gaze traveled upward, it connected with the bluest pair of eyes she'd ever seen in her life. Set in a tanned face that showed evidence of plenty of outdoor time, they crinkled when her rescuer smiled and held out a large hand covered in scars. "You must be Dr. Fitzgerald. I'm Josh Kinley, your new boss's little brother."

He was hardly little, she thought. Well over six feet tall, he had the rangy build of someone who spent his days working hard. Wearing a wide-open expression and a quick smile, he was nothing like the pale, stressed-out men she'd spent most of the last few years with. Then again, they'd all been studying their brains out, just like her. "I wasn't expecting a welcoming committee, but it's nice to meet you."

"Same here. The rescue center's been without a bona fide vet for over a year now. We're all real glad you accepted Erin's offer to come down here."

"It's a great situation for me, too. Especially since it included an apartment." Sure, it was above a pet supply store called Pampered Paws, but it had two bedrooms and would have come furnished if she hadn't had her own furniture. That reminded her of her current predicament, and she cast a look over her shoulder at her neatly labeled boxes, sitting just out of reach in the back of the truck. So close, and yet so far—that seemed to be the story of her life these days. "For now, I have to figure out how to get our stuff unloaded so this man can leave on time."

"I might be able to help you with that."

"How? Some of that furniture is pretty heavy."

"No doubt." Giving her a you-can-count-on-me grin, he sauntered over to where the driver was standing with his hands in his pockets. "So, where'd you start out this morning?"

"Louisville. Why?"

"That's a ways from here. You'll find the

best breakfast in three counties at the Oaks Café," Josh replied smoothly, nodding toward the restaurant next door. "Give us half an hour, and your meal's on me."

"Well…" Thinking it over, the mover scratched his thumb over his chin. "Okay. Thanks."

"You help me, I help you," Josh told him with a grin. "That's how we do things around here."

Exactly why she'd taken this job, Heather mused as the driver waved on his way into the diner. Her job at a prestigious Detroit clinic had been a dream come true, but Bailey had been raised in a small town and hadn't adjusted well to the culture shock of living in such an urban area. Although she hated to give up what she'd worked so hard to achieve, Heather instinctively knew that her niece would do best in the kind of environment she was accustomed to, surrounded by good, honest people who not only knew their neighbors but cared about what happened to them and their children.

It was the kind of childhood she and Craig had enjoyed. Thinking of her older brother still made her sad. As much as she missed him, she couldn't begin to imagine how hard it was for

Bailey, who'd lost her mother so young, he was the only parent she remembered having.

"Are you okay?" Josh asked, his brow creasing in a frown.

Oh, he was a sweetheart, this tall country boy with the rugged good looks. If she hadn't been totally consumed with learning how to be a single parent and settling into her new position, he was exactly the kind of guy she could have gone for in a major way. But life was what it was, and Heather had no intention of allowing herself to get waylaid by distractions, no matter how hunky they might be.

"I'm just trying to figure out what you have in mind," she said. "I'm no expert, but it seems to me that half an hour isn't going to make much difference here."

"Well, now, that's where you're wrong." Flashing her a mischievous grin, he strolled into the same diner he'd just sent the driver to. A couple of minutes later, he came out with a tall, dark-haired man who looked less than friendly. In fact, he made Heather think of a grizzly bear.

"Heather Fitzgerald," Josh began, motioning from her to his friend, "this is Cam Stewart. Erin's husband and all-around muscle."

Cam made a disparaging noise but shook her

hand gently enough. "Welcome to Oaks Crossing. How are things going so far?"

"Fine, but our stuff arrived here earlier than I expected, and the movers I originally scheduled for Wednesday are busy with other customers and can't get here until this afternoon. At the earliest," she added wryly.

"You hired movers?" Josh laughed. "What for?"

Mild as it was, the mocking didn't help her mood the slightest bit, and she bit her tongue to keep her simmering temper in check. "Erin said she'd try to find me some help, but I haven't heard back from her yet."

"I got nothing better to do just now." Looking at Cam, he grinned. "Gimme a hand?"

"Why not? It'll save me from mopping up the gallon of ketchup my new waitress just spilled in the storeroom."

"Good deal. Heather, can you work the door for us?"

And just like that, she had all the help she could ask for. "The boxes are labeled. Would it be too much trouble for you guys to put them in the right rooms?"

"No trouble at all," Josh assured her. That got him a menacing look from his friend before Cam hauled himself into the back of the moving truck. "Don't mind him. His bark is worse than his bite."

Punctuated by a broad wink, the old cliché made her difficult morning a little easier to take. "Did you just make a veterinarian joke?"

"That depends. Did you like it?"

His playful expression made her think of a big puppy whose only goal in life is to make everyone he comes across love him. At twenty-six, she'd spent many years with serious students determined to do everything in their power to make themselves successful. At the time, she'd assumed those days would be the most difficult she'd have to endure for a long time to come. But now, they paled in comparison to losing her only sibling and becoming an instant parent to a grieving child.

Despite what he'd told her, she recognized that Josh was going out of his way to lighten her mood, and she didn't want him to think she was standoffish. On the other hand, she didn't want to mislead him, either. Aside from being a nice guy, he was her boss's brother. She was keenly aware that her current employment situation was tenuous at best, and she couldn't afford to have any misunderstandings between them.

Stepping closer, she said in a quiet voice, "I know you're just being friendly, but I've got a lot on my plate right now. I don't have the time or the energy for anything else."

After a moment, he gave her a lazy grin. "Meaning me?"

"Yes. I'm not sure what you're after, but trust me—you're better off looking for it somewhere else."

"I'm not after anything, darlin'," he informed her in the slow, easy drawl that must make other women drool all over his scuffed work boots. "Just a smile. I'm thinking even a busy lady like you might have the time and the energy to give me one of those."

That he'd perfectly echoed her earlier comment impressed her to no end. Because of her looks, most men treated her like a miniature Barbie doll and never even considered the possibility that she had a brain and ideas that might be worth listening to. She could probably tell many of them the true meaning of life and they wouldn't register a single word she said.

Apparently, Josh Kinley was a different sort altogether. And since he'd been so great to a stressed-out woman he'd just met, she decided it was okay to offer him the smile he'd asked her for.

"There it is," he approved, returning it with

a blinding one of his own. "Just made my whole day."

He took over unloading the large truck with an efficiency that suggested to her that this wasn't the first time he'd managed such a big job. She manned the outer door, watching the two men thread through the pet store shelving, carrying furniture and boxes as if they handled this kind of assignment every day.

When the driver returned, her section of the truck was empty, and he was much more cheerful than he'd been when he'd first arrived. He handed her a copy of her receipt and even touched the bill of his baseball hat when she tipped him. "That's real nice of you, miss. You and your niece have a good day, now."

Heather could hardly believe this was the same surly man who'd pulled up half an hour ago and had been a whisker away from taking off with all her worldly possessions. When she said as much to Josh, he shrugged. "When you treat folks well, they do the same for you. Mostly, he looked hungry, so I bought him breakfast. No big deal."

"It was for me," she corrected him. Fishing a couple of twenties out of her wallet, she held one out to each of them. "You two really saved me this morning. Thank you."

"Just tell my wife I pitched in," Cam suggested. "We'll call it even."

She agreed, and he clapped Josh on the back before heading back into the restaurant. Still holding the money, she looked up at her rescuer. "Please let me pay you."

"I got my smile," he reminded her, blue eyes twinkling in fun.

"That's not nearly enough for the amount of work you did."

"Well, now, I guess that depends on the smile, doesn't it?"

This charming country boy was hard to resist, but she'd been schooled by men far more calculating than him. Calling up what she called her bad-news face, she replied, "I suppose so."

The cool gesture seemed to make no dent in his sunny disposition, and he went on as if she hadn't just shot him down. "Now that your stuff is off the sidewalk, I figure you're going out to the rescue center. I'm headed that way myself, so you can follow me if you want."

"I have a navigation system in my car," she informed him politely.

"Yeah, that might not work so far out of town if you lose the signal. But I'm sure a smart cookie like you can find the clinic on your own."

That didn't sound promising to her, and she found herself missing the convenience of street signs that directed people to where they wanted to go. Pushing the thought aside with a mental sigh, she decided not to make a challenging day even worse by being late for her first day of work. "On second thought, it might be best if I follow you. Thanks."

"Anytime."

He flashed her another grin and headed for a double-cab green pickup sporting the logo from his shirt on the driver's door. He climbed inside and reached down to adjust the radio before starting the engine and pulling out onto Main Street. As she watched him drive away accompanied by a honky-tonk tune, Heather wasn't entirely certain what had just happened. Putting away her money, she got into her car and prepared to play follow-the-leader.

Having spent so many years living in metropolitan areas, Heather had grown accustomed to traveling a certain number of blocks, turning at this light and that numbered avenue. This morning's commute was something completely foreign to her. The small business district gave way to a string of old homes surrounded by large yards whose neighbors hadn't bothered to put up fences to separate one plot from the next. The result was a pleasant blending of lawns and gardens, giving the town a picturesque country vibe even a devoted city girl like Heather could appreciate.

As they drove farther from town, the homes grew sparser, and she admired the lush countryside dominated by expansive farms that had been carved out of rolling acres of bluegrass and wildflowers. When they reached the sign for Gallimore Stables, she glanced out to take in the scope of the property Josh's family owned. Traditional white fences stretched as far as she could see, framing horses and ponies of every size and color. At the end of a gravel drive, a large white farmhouse with a wraparound porch beckoned visitors to stop and visit for a while. Erin had told her that the place had been in the Kinley family for generations, and despite some serious financial setbacks, they were all doing everything in their power to keep it that way.

Heather hadn't seen her childhood home since her parents had sold it to fund an early retirement traveling the world. She couldn't imagine what it would be like to be so connected to a piece of your family's history, being there year after year, building memories that would last beyond your own lifetime. That was what she wanted for Bailey, as much as for herself. A place to belong, where they'd always feel at home.

Hopefully, putting aside her old dreams and coming to Oaks Crossing would prove to be the first step to a better life for both of them.

Heather Fitzgerald wasn't at all what Josh had been expecting.

With a cloud of curly blond hair and a killer pair of baby blues, the petite vet looked more like a shoe-in for prom queen than someone capable of managing sick and injured animals. Then again, he spent his days wrestling with cranky field hands, tractors and harvesters, working sunup to sundown to wring every ounce of profit out of his end of their struggling horse farm. It didn't leave him much spare time for pondering what made folks tick.

As so many Kinleys before him had done, when it rained too much, he stared at the sky and prayed for the sun to come out again. And when the soil got too dry, he prayed for rain, season by season, methodically rotating the crops in each field to keep the fertile acreage as productive as it could possibly be. It wasn't an easy life, but the land was like a member of the family to him, and he loved it with everything he had.

Many of his childhood friends had moved

away after graduation, but at twenty-seven, Josh couldn't envision being truly happy anywhere else. If only his high school sweetheart, Cindy O'Donnell, had felt the same way, he'd be married and a father by now. Sadly, she'd left him behind to strike out on her own, and he'd finally come to realize that, much as he'd loved her, they simply weren't meant for each other.

Ever since he could remember, he'd known that this was where he belonged. While so many people fretted over where to go and what to do, he sat back and listened to them, grateful that he'd been planted in the right place. All he needed to make his life complete was a family of his own. More than anything, he wanted the kind of strong marriage his parents had built together, something that would last through the good times and the bad. But since losing Cindy to the big, bad world, he'd gone through enough failed relationships to know that wanting something wasn't enough. You had to make it happen.

His two older brothers were happily married now, and they'd both told him the secret was to find a woman capable of loving him for who he was. Unfortunately for him, their advice had ended there, leaving him as clueless as ever.

Josh checked his rearview mirror to make

sure Heather was still with him before taking the fork that snaked through the woods on its way to the clinic. She matched the maneuver, and before long they pulled into the gravel lot in front of the Oaks Crossing Rescue Center. Located on a few acres at the edge of the main farm, it was surrounded by trees and unspoiled meadow, the perfect spot for a place devoted to caring for animals.

He pulled in and parked off to the side to leave a closer space for Heather's car. She was the doc, he reasoned, so she deserved the VIP treatment. Now that he thought about it, they should designate a spot for her so visitors and volunteers didn't block her entrance if she had to come in quickly and take care of an emergency.

Josh got out of his truck and strolled toward the main building, assessing the best place for her to park in the future. When she arrived and stepped out of her car, he heard her call out his name. "Did you lose something?"

"Just thinkin'," he replied, and he pointed to the pavement in front of the clinic while he explained.

He'd expected her to be on board with the perk, maybe even a little flattered that he'd thought of it. But she surprised him by shaking her head. "That's really not necessary. Anywhere is fine."

She'd initially struck him as a bit of a princess, accustomed to having people help her at the drop of a hat. That she actually seemed to have an independent streak was a pleasant surprise to him. "Okay. Let me know if you change your mind."

"I won't, but I appreciate the offer."

There was that prim, overly polite tone again. Easygoing by nature, Josh normally accepted people as they were, figuring it was their right to choose their own attitudes. But he had to admit that her rapid shifts from sweet to stern were beginning to bug him. Add that to the fact that she'd all but ordered him to back off earlier, and he counted two strikes.

And everyone knew you got only three.

Unwilling to blow them all at once, he put aside his curiosity about the pretty veterinarian and motioned her toward the glass front door etched with the clinic's logo. "Ladies first."

She gave him a long, uncomfortable look that made him feel like a new species of bug. Finally, the cynical glint in her eyes mellowed, and she offered him a tentative smile. "Thank you."

"Anytime."

That got him another clinical stare. "You

said that before, when we were in town. You really mean it, don't you?"

"Wouldn't say it if I didn't."

"In my experience, most guys aren't that honest."

"Well, ma'am," he responded in his best down-home accent, "I think you'll find we do things a little differently around here."

"I've never lived anywhere other than Michigan," she confided. "I guess I have some things to learn about how things work in Kentucky."

Josh had no doubt that before long she'd have men lined up to give her a few lessons on the subject. Not him, of course, he thought with a muted grin. She'd made it plain that she wasn't interested in him. While he didn't understand her chilly behavior toward him, he'd been raised to have a healthy respect for women. Especially the feisty ones.

When he realized she still hadn't made a move to go inside, he turned to her with a sympathetic smile. "Nervous?"

"A bit." Peering into the vacant lobby, she frowned in concern. "This is my first time being in charge of a veterinary practice, and I'm not sure what to expect."

In her confession, Josh heard that she wasn't worried about the actual doctoring, but about handling the people involved. Inspiration struck, and he said, "Around here, we get some of every critter around. How 'bout a tour of the animals before you meet the staff?"

"Are you sure? I mean, don't you have other things to do?"

Josh had never had to contend with a nerve-racking first day on the job, or moving with a child hundreds of miles from the only home he'd ever known. But he could imagine it was pretty intimidating, even for this intelligent woman making a career in such a challenging field. His late father had taught them all that a little patience went a long way with most creatures, whether they were the four-legged or the two-legged kind. "Yeah, but they can wait a while longer."

He skirted the kennel building and took her out to where temporary corrals held an interesting collection of wild animals healing before being released back into the forest. Today, the group included a mother duck with a broken wing and her fuzzy yellow brood of ten, an injured armadillo and a llama that had escaped from somewhere and taken up residence in a local farmer's herd of dairy cows.

As they strolled along the enclosure, Josh filled her in on how each animal had come to be here and what he knew of the plans to rehabilitate and release them back to their homes.

While he was talking, a new arrival ambled over and eyed them with obvious curiosity.

Heather's eyes just about popped out of her head. "Is that a bear cub?"

"Yeah. My niece and nephew named him Teddy. You've never seen one?"

"Sure, in zoos and on TV. Never up close like this." She glanced around and said, "Mama bears don't normally stand by and just let you scoop up their babies. I wonder where she is."

Josh had a hunch about what had happened to the absent mother, but he kept his mouth shut to avoid distressing this lovely city girl with one of the less appealing facts of country life. But she was a sharp woman, and after thinking on it for a few moments, she frowned. "Hunters, right?"

"That'd be my guess. Bears are pretty smart, so they don't tangle with cars, and not many big trucks come through here."

"What a shame," she commented sadly, hunkering down to greet the orphaned cub that was coming to the rail of his enclosure to check them out. Unlike many folks who visited, she was smart enough not to reach through the fence to pet him. In spite of her caution, Josh had no trouble picking up on her sympathy for Teddy. Apparently, neither did the bear, which sidled over and gazed curiously at her. "What's going to happen to this poor baby?"

"There's a wildlife rehabilitator who works here as a volunteer. She'll figure out what he needs and make sure he can take care of himself when they let him go."

Heather stood and faced Josh, interest lighting her eyes. "You seem to know a lot about this place. I thought you were in charge of the farm."

Josh couldn't keep back a laugh. "Not hardly. Big brother Mike runs the horse training business, and Drew's our foreman when it comes to the farmwork. I manage the fields and try not to lose us too much money."

When he laid it out that way, he realized that his job didn't sound like much, but it had taken up most of his waking hours since he was ten years old. While he didn't usually dwell on the impression he made on folks, he couldn't help wondering what this highly educated woman thought of his very simple existence.

"I've never lived on a farm myself, but I think there's a lot more to it than that."

Josh pretended to consider her comment before shaking his head. "Nope. That pretty much sums it up. Works for me, though. I like keeping things uncomplicated."

"So do I," she agreed with a quick laugh.

"Unfortunately, in my world they never seem to stay that way."

"You're talking about your niece?" She nodded, and he took the opportunity to find out more about her. "Mind if I ask what happened?"

"There's not that much to tell. When Bailey was two, her mother, Polly, died from complications after an operation. My brother Craig had his hands full working and being a single dad. Bailey was visiting me this past February, and I got a call from the Michigan State Police." Her chin began to tremble, and she paused for a deep breath before going on. "Craig's car hit a patch of ice and ran straight into a bridge support on the interstate. He died on impact, and Bailey's life changed forever."

"And yours," Josh added somberly. That explained her immediate connection to Teddy. An orphan like Bailey, he was alone in the world and needed someone to take care of him until he could fend for himself.

"I love her to pieces," Heather murmured with a gentle smile. "But she's still lost without her daddy. It breaks my heart to see her suffering, and I wish there was more I could do to help her."

"I'm not a dad myself, but from what I've seen in my own family, kids need love and attention more than anything. Give her those and some time, and she'll be okay."

She stared up at him in obvious amazement. "That's incredibly good advice."

"You sound surprised."

"I am, and that almost never happens."

Heather eyed Josh with the kind of respect he seldom received. Being the youngest Kinley, and laid-back to boot, meant that folks often didn't take him seriously. This pragmatic woman, with her quick mind and gorgeous blue eyes, had apparently noticed something in him that most people missed.

It seemed to him that there was more to this jaded city girl than met the eye. And he was just intrigued enough to wonder if she might eventually give him the chance to get to know her better.

Chapter Two

The guided tour gave Heather an opportunity to get her bearings and develop a sense of the place where she'd be working. Huge oak trees outlined the clearing that housed the clinic, kennel and a couple of barns that Josh had explained were reserved for injured wild animals that people had brought in for care. A structure with several brand-new sections of lumber amid more weathered planks caught her eye, and she asked, "What's back there?"

"Feed and bedding storage," he explained in a somber tone. "We had a bad fire in there last fall, but fortunately my sister-in-law Bekah was here to sound the alarm, and no one was hurt. Now there's a fire detection and sprinkler system, but the staff decided that it's still a good idea to keep the dry stuff away from the animals."

"That makes sense."

"So, that's everything out here. Ready to go in and meet the rest of your crew?"

"Sounds good," she responded, hoping she sounded confident and dependable. She might be the new kid in town, but she was a full-fledged veterinarian now, and she was more than capable of managing a small clinic like this. At least, that's what she wanted everyone to believe. If any of them suspected that she was a step short of terrified, they'd never give her the respect she needed if she was going to be effective. Not to mention, she didn't want anyone expressing any doubts to their boss. Succeeding here was crucial for Bailey, and unusual as this assignment might be, Heather knew she'd have to find a way to make it work.

From Josh's long, assessing look, she realized that despite his casual manner and country boy grin, he wasn't the least bit fooled by her bravado. She waited for him to call her out, but instead he gave her an understanding smile. "Would you like me to stick around and introduce you to everyone?"

She had to admit she liked the way he asked her for her approval rather than simply bulldozing ahead. So many people—especially men—took one look at her and assumed that she wasn't capable of managing difficult situations on her own. Stumbling across a guy who thought otherwise was a wonderful surprise. "That would be nice. Thank you."

"Not a problem. First days are tough."

He strolled past her to open the door and stepped aside to let her go in first. Bolstered by his encouraging words, she walked through it feeling prepared for whatever might await her on the other side. The lobby was no longer empty, and when she saw what was going on, her confidence began to waver.

There, on a blanket in the middle of the floor, lay a motionless cat that had obviously been hit by a car. As if that wasn't heart-wrenching enough, two women were sitting cross-legged beside her, staring down at something she couldn't see. Edging closer to avoid startling anyone, Heather understood why.

Three tiny kittens were curled up in a towel stretched across one of the nurse's laps, eyes closed while they mewed silently, hunting for their mother. The other woman was cooing at another set of four, gently stroking them while they cried. At one point, she lifted her shoulder, wiping tears from her cheeks with the sleeve of her blood-stained T-shirt.

Finally, she sat back with the tiniest kitten Heather had ever seen cuddled against her chest. "I count eight altogether, Bekah. How are yours doing?"

"Shaky but still with us," the other woman replied in a sad voice. "I don't know how you managed to save all these babies, Sierra."

"God wanted all of them to make it, so He made sure they were on the side of the road where I'd see them," she commented, touching noses with the tiny creature in her arms. "I just wish we could've saved your mama for you, little one."

"Awesome job, you two," Josh approved quietly. "And you couldn't have arranged a better way to impress our new vet if you'd tried."

The two women traded a shocked glance before looking up at her, and Heather realized they'd been so focused on their patients, they hadn't noticed her come in. Instantly, she knew she was in the right place. She'd have no trouble working with people who were that devoted to the animals they cared for.

"Don't let me interrupt what you're doing. But if you'd like a hand, I'll be happy to help."

"Sierra Walker, Bekah Kinley, this is Heather Fitzgerald." Josh made the introductions, pointing each of them out as he spoke so they'd know who was who. Then he knelt to gently wrap the dead cat inside the blanket. "You ladies tend to the babies while I take Mom out back to the pet cemetery and find a nice spot for her."

After he'd gone, Heather felt a little lost. Falling back on years of crisis training, she summoned a helpful smile and asked, "What would you like me to do first?"

"If you can take this one," Sierra replied, handing off the helpless scrap of fur, "Bekah and I can scoop up the rest, and we'll take them all back to the nursery."

A quick peek told Heather the kitten she held was a female, and she instinctively brought the small cat into her neck where it could snuggle against her warm skin. The fuzzy darling nosed its way into a dangling lock of Heather's hair and let out a sigh that would have shattered a heart made of granite. Heather followed the other two women into a small room whose floor was occupied by nests made from flannel sheets and soft blankets.

They settled the litter of kittens in one of the cocoons together, and Heather sat down to get a better look at them. Their colors ran the spectrum of browns from tiger to calico, ranging in size from small to downright tiny. If any of them weighed a pound, she'd be astounded. Not wanting to disturb them any more than necessary, she lightly passed a hand over each one, feeling for injuries or labored breathing that would indicate distress.

The seven larger ones seemed more or less stable, and they clustered together in a warm lump, using each other for pillows. The runt didn't seem even remotely interested in joining the group, and she collapsed in an exhausted pile at the edge of their nest, her face pinched and her delicate frame shuddering with every shallow breath.

"I don't like the looks of this one," Heather commented somberly. "Do you have an incubator?"

"Sort of." Sierra half closed the door and took something from a hook attached to the back. She held it out with a grin. "It's a sling they sell for mothers of preemies. The fabric is soft and light enough to let them breathe. I've found it works well for critter babies, too."

"What a great idea. If you don't mind, we can take turns with it."

"You want to papoose a kitten while you're working?" Bekah asked.

Heather answered by pulling on the hammock-like device and carefully setting her frail charge inside. "She's not that heavy, so as long as I'm not seeing patients, I can manage."

"I've never met a vet who'd even think of

doing that," Sierra informed her with a smile. "I think we're gonna get along just fine."

The quick, heartfelt approval chased off the last of Heather's lingering nervousness. "We're more than just coworkers here. We're a team, and everyone should pull their own weight, including me."

"Of course, these days some of us have more weight to pull than others," Bekah joked, smoothing her hands over a modest baby bump. The rings sparkling on her left hand caught Heather's eye, and she felt a twinge of envy for the pretty young mother-to-be. Then again, she reminded herself, she'd chosen to postpone having children until after she was firmly established in her own veterinary practice. It was a logical decision, and she was comfortable with the choice she'd made.

Most of the time.

"Will we be throwing you a baby shower soon?" Heather asked.

"I'm not due until August, so it'll be a while still."

"What are your plans after that?"

"I'd like to keep working here, but that will depend on the baby," she answered truthfully. "Family first."

"Absolutely," Heather agreed, fearing that she might have overstepped her professional boundaries. Most people she'd worked with were stiffly polite, not open and friendly like these two. Now that she thought about it, Josh and Cam had made her feel right at home, too. Apparently, the residents of this small Kentucky town were the warm, welcoming type. This made her hopeful that Bailey would enjoy Oaks Crossing more than she had Detroit.

"Speaking of family," Sierra said while she mixed kitten formula in a container, "Erin told us you have a niece who lives with you. Does she like animals?"

"Loves them. She's settling in at the day care in town, but I'm planning to bring her to work with me sometime next week to see the menagerie we've got here. I'll have to make sure she never sees this little darling, though," she added, ticking the sleeping kitten's pink nose with her fingertip. "I'm afraid if that happened, we'd end up keeping her."

"Occupational hazard." Sierra chuckled. "If my landlord allowed pets, I'd have a dozen of them."

"When they're old enough, Erin will take them to Pampered Paws and display them in the front window," Bekah assured her, rubbing the striped forehead gently. "These cuties won't last more than a few days there."

It hadn't occurred to Heather that living

above the pet store would mean that she and Bailey would be walking past adorable babies every day. While she was practical enough to bypass the temptation, she wasn't sure that a five-year-old would understand why they couldn't adopt some of their furry visitors.

Then again, if they already had a cat, she'd have a built-in excuse to say no to more. It couldn't hurt to think about it, anyway. A pet might also coax Bailey out of her shell and help her adjust to her new home more quickly. Because Heather wasn't used to worrying about anything other than her job, she felt very out of her element trying to help her troubled niece.

While she was debating, Josh poked his head in through the open top half of the Dutch door. "Everything good in here?"

"More or less," Sierra replied while she filled small bottles and capped them with even smaller rubber nipples. "We could use an extra set of hands, though. Have you got time?"

He sent Heather a questioning look, which she didn't understand. Then it occurred to her that while she considered herself an outsider, the others already viewed her as being in charge of the clinic. It didn't feel quite right to her, but she assumed she'd get used to it. Eventually.

"The more the merrier," she said.

"My mom always says that," he commented as he joined them, closing the door to keep anyone from escaping.

"Mine, too," Heather told him with a smile. "That's how my dad ended up starting out his retirement touring Europe in an RV with her, a Pomeranian and four parakeets."

"Sounds loud." Josh chuckled, taking a bottle from the counter before sitting on the floor beside the kittens. His long legs stretched out in front of him, he lifted a bawling tiger and cradled it against him in a practiced motion.

The small room didn't have much space for spreading out, so Heather resigned herself to settling next to him with a bottle of her own. "I'm guessing you've done this before."

"Everyone in the family likes to help out down here when we can. Except Mike," he added with a grin. "Our Kentucky cowboy's got his hands full wrangling all those horses."

"I noticed them in the fields when we were driving out here. It looks like you have everything from Thoroughbreds to Shetland ponies."

"My great-grandfather started out training horses for the military in World War I, then Dad trained racehorses. After he passed away, that business disappeared and we came pretty close to losing the farm. Mike's kind of a horse whisperer, and he came up with the idea to school retired racehorses and sell them to folks for riding."

"What about the others? I saw a Belgian in the front pasture, grazing next to an Arabian."

"Mike rescues some from bad situations, others come from owners who can't keep 'em anymore and want them to have a good home. If they don't get adopted, they stay here with us," he added, grinning down at the slurping kitten. "We're just a bunch of softies around here, aren't we?"

Heather smiled at the sight of the tall, brawny farmer cuddling the helpless animal, speaking to it in the kind of gentle tone most people reserved for children. While she had no intention of complicating her life any further right now, she couldn't deny that he had a special brand of bright, sunny charm.

It was a good thing she'd already committed to staying single for the sake of Bailey and her career. Otherwise, Josh Kinley might have proved to be impossible to resist.

"Hello?"

It was Thursday afternoon, and Josh was buried underneath the oldest tractor in the county, trying to wrestle the drive belt back into place, when he heard a now-familiar voice. Hauling himself out hand over hand, he looked up to find Heather staring down at him with an amused look on her face.

"Hey there, Doc. What brings you out here?"

"It's my lunch hour, so I decided to go exploring." She looked around her at the overgrown field, out toward the neatly plowed acreage in the distance, and then back at him. "I'm not an agricultural expert, but this looks like it's pretty far from where you've been working. Do you mind if I ask what you're doing?"

The crop portion of the farm was his domain. His brothers and their few hired hands were fully occupied with the horses, so Josh was used to doing his own thing without anyone questioning him. As much a part of him as his blue eyes, these rolling hills were the legacy Josh hoped to pass along to his own children someday.

Lately, though, the red numbers had been sinking lower by the month, no matter how hard they all worked. If they didn't come up with something brilliant to bring in some cash on a regular basis, they'd be forced to sell off chunks of land for the first time in the farm's long history. And that would be the beginning of the end for Gallimore Stables.

Josh was known as the upbeat one in the family, and for their sake he kept his outlook rosy. But even a determined optimist like him had to acknowledge that something concrete needed to be done, and quickly. So he'd devised a plan but hadn't told anyone, not even Mom. But he'd been dying to share it with someone, and since it didn't impact her directly, Heather seemed like a good choice.

"Well, I could tell you," he said with a grin, "but you have to keep it to yourself."

Enthusiasm sparkled in her eyes, and she nodded. "I promise."

After describing the circumstances to her, he explained what he was up to. "So, I did some research and found out that a lot of corn in Kentucky is sold to the ethanol market. To be made into gasoline."

"I know what ethanol is," she informed him tartly.

Smothering a grin, he went on. "I got the idea when my nephew Parker built a biodiesel engine for a science fair. I had let this section go fallow to rest, so it was ready for planting this year. I'm just putting in a different kind of corn this time, and then I'll pray the prices stay where they are till harvest time."

"That's a good idea. I hope it works out the way you want it to."

Her cautious tone made him frown. "You

sound like someone who has some experience with plans going awry."

"More than I'd like," she admitted softly, as if she hated to confide that to him. Uncertainty darkened her eyes before giving way to the cool look he'd noticed earlier. "When I saw you over here I thought I'd come see if I could help somehow."

Josh glanced over her neat blouse and trousers, down to the sensible but pretty shoes she was wearing. "You sure about that?"

"I might be a city girl, but I'm no stranger to dirt. Besides, I owe you for the time you spent with the moving van and all those kittens the other day. What can I do?"

She seemed bound and determined to lend him a hand, so Josh hunted for something she could do that wouldn't leave her either filthy or hurt. "Well, I guess you could brace this for me—" he grasped the shifter "—while I rethread the belt onto the pulleys."

"I have no idea what you're talking about," she admitted with a cute half grin, "but I understand the bracing part. Just let me know when I should let go."

"Will do."

As he slid back underneath the ancient machine they called The Beast, Josh couldn't keep from wondering if a walk was all that had brought her so far from the center. While he maneuvered the pieces back into alignment, he asked, "So how're you getting along down there?"

"Fine. I'm learning about the animals a few at a time. Bekah's wonderful with them, and Sierra's very knowledgeable about everything."

Josh picked up on the annoyance edging her tone and chuckled through the clanking of his wrench. "Yeah, she's kinda bossy. I think that's why Erin hired her. They've got the same charge-ahead approach to stuff."

"So, you're the youngest in your family?" When he grunted a reply, she went on. "I was, too. It's not easy, is it?"

She was getting at something, but Josh had no clue what it might be. Distracted by his fascinating visitor, he lost his grip on the belt and the entire pulley system let go, jamming his hand against the rusty metal housing. Biting back a curse, he scrambled free to check the damage.

"Oh, that looks bad," Heather announced, crouching down for a closer inspection of his hand. Then she gave him a knowing look. "You're thinking something really bad right now, aren't you?"

"Yeah. Don't tell my mom."

"Tell her what?" Heather teased, adding a

wink. So far, she'd given him the impression that she was a fairly serious person. Coming from her, the playful gesture seemed out of place, but he welcomed the glimpse of her lighter side. Maybe the classy vet wasn't so prim and proper, after all. "I'm assuming this kind of thing happens a lot on a farm. Do you have a first aid kit?"

"Behind the seat."

She climbed up the metal steps and unhooked the faded red case that hung from a set of rusty hooks. When she rejoined him, she opened it and eyed the scant contents with a doubtful expression. Picking up a tube of antibacterial ointment, she squinted at it before giving him a chiding look. "This expired five years ago."

"Huh. How 'bout that?" That made her glare, and he held up his uninjured hand in a placating gesture. "Don't blame me. Most of the time, I just wrap a bandanna around something like this and keep on working."

"It's a wonder you've never gotten an infection. Or tetanus," she added ominously, eyeing the bleeding gashes on his hand.

"I got my shot."

Again with the suspicious stare. "When?"

He had no idea. His years drifted from season to season, dictated more by what was going on around the farm than by the calendar. When you spent most of your life waking with the sun and finishing in the glare of tractor headlights, it was easy to lose track of pretty much everything else. To his mind, one of the best inventions ever was the automated payment system. Ever since Bekah had walked him through covering his handful of bills that way, he hadn't missed a single payment. It was awesome.

"That's what I thought," Heather continued, adding a sigh that made it clear he wasn't the first person she'd run across who ignored what she considered to be the important things. Glancing around, she stopped when she noticed something in the distance. "Is that a house?"

"Yeah, it's mine. Why?"

"I don't suppose you have something there to get this cleaned up properly?"

"'Course I do," he retorted. "I'm not a moron."

"Good. We'll do what we can there and then you should get to the nearest clinic. You really need to have that looked at by a doctor."

"You're a doctor."

"A people doctor," she corrected him in a clipped, don't-mess-with-me tone. "I can do the basics, but this needs to be stitched, and you need a specialist for that. You shouldn't take injuries like this lightly, Josh. They can get worse in a hurry."

Normally, he hated being lectured as if he were a troublesome child, but this one came in a voice laced with genuine concern. Realizing that this compassionate woman meant well, he put aside his aversion to being told what to do and nodded. "Okay, but that storm's coming in real fast, and I wanna finish plowing this section before it starts raining. I'll go into town to see Doc Sheppard when I'm finished."

"You'll go now," she insisted, glowering at him. When he glowered back, she gave him a wry smile. "Or I'll tell your mom."

"You haven't even met her yet."

"Imagine how awkward that would be for all of us. 'Hello, Mrs. Kinley, nice to meet you. By the way, your youngest son is a stubborn mule who cares more about working over a few extra acres than taking care of his health. I just thought you'd like to know.'"

"All right, I get it. Man, you're a pain," he added as he got to his feet and glared down at her.

"That won't work on me, country boy," she informed him airily as she rose to stand. "I've seen the business end of an angry bull up close, so you don't scare me."

Brushing past him, she started off at a pace

quick enough that he had to hurry to catch up. Her legs were a lot shorter than his, so it took him only a few strides. "Why was he mad?"

"Who?"

"The bull," Josh pressed. "Was he mad at you or someone else?"

"Some genius trucked his favorite cow off to another farm while he was watching. They'd been together for years, and he didn't appreciate them taking her away from him."

Her perception of the animal's emotions impressed him. Petite as she was, mothering a helpless kitten had seemed like a natural fit. It should have been a real stretch for him to picture her facing down a raging bull, but for some reason he had no trouble envisioning it. Maybe it was the spunky attitude she'd shown, or her no-nonsense approach to his injury.

Or maybe it was something else completely. Since he'd never met anyone like Heather, he had no frame of reference to enable him to make that kind of judgment. So he did what he usually did when he was perplexed by an unanswerable question. Put it out of his mind and moved on.

"How are the kittens doing?"

"The bigger ones seem comfortable enough, but the tiniest one worries me. She doesn't seem to feel connected to them at all."

"Maybe she's not." Heather gave him a quizzical look, and he explained. "This time of year, there're lots of new kittens around, either in people's outbuildings or the woods. The mothers instinctively move them from spot to spot, and it's not uncommon for one of them to get hit. If the kittens are out in the open, someone will bring them in to the center like Sierra did today."

"Do you have a lot of barn cats on the farm?"

"About a dozen, I'd guess. They're great for rodent control, so we're happy to have 'em."

"Are they catchable?"

"I guess we could figure out a way to get ahold of them," he replied. "Why?"

"If we neuter them and give them some basic vaccines, they won't add to the feral population, and the ones you have won't pass along any nasty diseases."

"Huh. I never thought of that."

"Most people don't," she commented sadly. "In rural towns like this, you don't even notice wild cats because there are so many places for them to hide. But many of them are sick, and they keep adding to their numbers until the health of the entire population is compromised. You don't hear anything about it until a rabid stray bites a person, and then it's all over the news for a few days before some other story takes over."

The bitterness in her tone got his attention more than the words. "It sounds like you've been up on this soapbox before."

"For all the good it's done," she said bitterly. "The last clinic I worked at during my residency, they called me the 'crazy cat lady,' and not in a nice way."

"Gave them a reason to ignore you."

"Yes," she acknowledged with a shocked expression. "How did you guess?"

"Happens all the time when someone has the nerve to buck the system. If folks can write a crusader off as nutty, they can ignore the problem. I just can't imagine anyone doing it to someone as smart as you."

Heather had given him plenty of looks in the short time they'd been acquainted with each other, but this was one he hadn't seen yet. Shining in those incredible eyes was a combination of gratitude and astonishment. He wasn't sure what that meant, but she'd finally quit glaring at him, so he figured that was a good sign.

"You think I'm smart?" When he nodded, she shook her head with a quick laugh. "Most guys can't see past the blond hair and blue eyes. What makes you so different?"

"Don't get me wrong," he was quick to correct her, "you're cute as a button. But Erin threatened me with grave bodily harm if I even thought about making a play for you."

"Really?" Now those eyes gleamed with something he'd seen plenty of in his lifetime: feminine interest. "And if she hadn't?"

"We'd be having dinner tonight."

For some reason, she laughed. "Oh, you're a real piece of work, country boy. What makes you think I'd say yes even if you were allowed to ask me out?"

"I don't know, darlin'," he drawled with a lazy grin. "Past experience?"

"You realize that sounds arrogant, right?"

"Confident," he corrected her smoothly as they arrived at the front porch of a light gray cottage with white shutters. "After all, I'm a Kinley boy."

"Meaning?"

Grinning, he went up the steps and opened the screen door for her. "Ask around town. I'm sure you'll find out all you wanna know."

"Please," she scoffed, rolling those gorgeous baby blues. "I'm too busy to waste my time with gossip. I'll just figure it out on my own."

"I take it that means you're planning to stay in Oaks Crossing awhile."

"It depends on how Bailey does here, so I'm

still working on that one. I guess we'll have to see."

"I guess we will."

His response got him another curious look, but she didn't say anything more as she went through the screen door he opened for her. Following her inside, he had to admit that Heather Fitzgerald was the most intriguing woman he'd ever run across. Nothing like the sweet, uncomplicated girls he preferred, she had the kind of depth a laid-back guy like him was probably safer admiring from a respectable distance.

It was a good thing Erin had proclaimed her off-limits, he mused with a grin. Otherwise, he might have been tempted to bridge that gap and discover what it was about her that made him want to break the rules.

Chapter Three

Heather went through Josh's front door and into a living room that clearly announced the owner wasn't around much. The couch and mismatched chairs looked old, the throw pillows were faded and the windows were unblocked by drapes. Through an open side door, she glimpsed a bedroom that looked as if it had recently been through a mini tornado.

In short, the single-story cottage was the very definition of a bachelor pad. Then she noticed the collection of framed pictures on the dusty mantel and walked over for a better look. The people in them bore an unmistakable resemblance to one another, and she smiled at the scenes of picnics and muddy backyard football games. In one, a much younger version of her new boss, Erin, was standing atop a pyramid, arms extended in triumph. Recognizing Josh on the bottom row, Heather asked, "How old were you in this one?"

"Oh, thirteen maybe. Those are my older brothers, Mike and Drew, on either side of me. Right after Mom got this shot, the foundation guys pulled out, and everyone but Erin landed in a pile on top of us. The princess ended up breaking her arm."

"That wasn't very nice of you."

Unfazed by her scolding, he chuckled. "You should've heard what she was yelling at the time. That wasn't very nice, either."

Heather hadn't met all the Kinleys yet, but from what she'd gathered, they were one of those big, raucous families that had a lot of fun together. She'd been so occupied by their move that getting acquainted with the rest of Erin's family hadn't been a priority for her before. But now Heather found herself looking forward to meeting the rest of the clan.

"All right," she said briskly, heading for the kitchen. "Let's get that hand cleaned up so you don't scare the doctor half to death when you show up at his office."

"I really can drive myself," Josh argued while she rummaged through a small bank of cupboards for a clean towel and some peroxide. "You don't have to babysit me like I'm ten."

Heather glanced out the window at his vintage green pickup and then gave him a raised-eyebrow look. "I'm guessing that monster has a standard transmission?"

"Yeah. So?"

In answer, she dabbed at the slice cutting across his palm that still hadn't stopped bleeding and held a thick gauze pad in place before wrapping a thin dish towel around his hand. Leveling a stern glare at this unexpectedly stubborn man, she announced, "You're not using this hand until it's been stitched and dressed by a professional. Period, end of story."

"You sound like my mom."

"Good, then I must be doing it right." Tying the makeshift bandage to keep it in place, she grabbed the keys from their hook by the back door. "Now, let's go. I have plenty of other patients waiting for me at the clinic."

In truth, she didn't know that for certain, but she was hoping that the softhearted farmer's affection for the animals would nudge him to get moving in the right direction. He didn't protest any further, which she was grateful for, and they walked out to his truck together. She wasn't used to dealing with patients who talked back, and it was more than a little unsettling.

This one surprised her by strolling to the driver's door and opening it for her. Considering the fact that he was probably miffed at her right now, the gentlemanly gesture made her smile. "Thank you."

"Sure. Doc Sheppard's on Main Street, up a ways from the Oaks Café, right across from the park. It's a big old Victorian, gray with a red front door and black trim around the windows. You can't miss it."

Armed with those directions, Heather engaged the clutch, dropped the truck into Reverse and stepped on the gas. With a stomach-rolling lurch, the pickup flew backward for several yards before her reflexes kicked in and she managed to slam on the brakes.

"Not a word," she cautioned, easing the shifter into first gear.

He obliged her, but she could almost feel him grinning at her. When she flicked a look toward him, he pulled a sober face that did nothing to mask the humor glinting in his eyes. Deciding to let her irritation go, she focused on moving through the gears on the old truck without shredding the transmission. By the time they got to town, she had the hang of it and parked in a small lot beside a graceful old home with a wrought iron signpost that read Henry Sheppard, MD.

"I'd love to have my office in a place like this someday," she commented while they walked to the side door marked for visitors. "The house itself is gorgeous, and he can't beat the commute to work."

"Yeah, it's pretty nice."

Once they were inside, she waited while Josh spoke to a receptionist who looked as if she might have been an original occupant of the stately home. "Hi, Mrs. Sheppard. Is the doc available?"

Tsking at him, the physician's wife came around the desk to frown at Josh's towel-wrapped hand. "Oh, that looks bad. What have you done this time?"

When he explained, she shook her head with a sympathetic expression. "You poor dear." Then she turned her attention to Heather, offering a slender hand. "You must be the new vet everyone's been buzzing about. I'm Louise Sheppard, otherwise known as the doc's wife. Welcome to Oaks Crossing."

Everyone? Heather echoed silently. She'd been here only a few days, and she was already the hot topic around town? In Detroit, she'd been just another face in a very large crowd, so she wasn't accustomed to being singled out this way. She did her best to summon a friendly smile. "Thank you."

"How does your niece like our day care?" the woman continued. "My daughter-in-law

Tammy started it over the winter, and she's thrilled to have another preschooler in the class."

"This is her first week there, but she seems to be doing fine. Shouldn't you be getting the doctor to have a look at Josh's hand?" she added as politely as she could.

"Of course. How silly of me to be rambling along when there's work to be done. You have a seat, and I'll go let Henry know you're here."

Within a few minutes, a plump woman was escorted into the waiting room by a tall, white-haired man wearing an open lab coat over a navy polo shirt and khakis. "You get that prescription filled," he told her, "and I'll be calling you tomorrow morning to see how that cough is. Meantime, get some rest and have your daughter make you that wonderful peach cobbler of hers. Best medicine around," he said with a wink that suggested he'd sampled the dessert himself.

The woman thanked him and beamed at Josh, who'd jumped up to hold the door open for her. "Such a good boy. Say hello to your mother for me."

"Will do, Mrs. Gilbert. Hope you're feeling better soon."

Covering her mouth with a lace-edged handkerchief, she coughed and held up a hand in farewell as she left. Once she was gone, the doctor turned to Josh with a stern look. "What have you done this time?"

Heather noticed that he'd repeated his wife's earlier question word for word, and she wondered how often Josh had been here with injuries over the years. With a sheepish look, Josh unwrapped his hand and stood patiently while the physician assessed the damage. Then the doctor did something that stunned Heather.

Angling a glance at her, he asked, "What do you think?"

She waited a beat so her surprise at being consulted wouldn't come across. "Several stitches will close up the wound itself. The metal was rusty, so if he's due for a tetanus booster, this would be a good time for it."

"My thoughts exactly." Nodding, he smiled proudly at her as if she were his star pupil. Foolish as it seemed, she felt a sense of pride at having earned the approval of such an experienced medical professional. "Come on back, son, and we'll get you fixed up in no time."

Suddenly, what had been a straight wind began to howl in the eaves of the old house, and Josh scowled at the ceiling. "That doesn't sound good."

"I've heard worse," Dr. Sheppard assured him on their way toward one of two examining rooms. "Just look at it this way—the rain will give you a day off to watch TV and rest your hand."

Josh grumbled a reply, but she didn't catch the words before the door closed behind him. Since she had the keys to his truck, Heather realized that she'd be waiting around until he was finished. So she took the opportunity to sit down and check in with the clinic.

"Hi, Sierra, it's Heather. My walk got interrupted by Josh hurting his hand, so I'm in town with him at Dr. Sheppard's. I shouldn't be much longer. Do you need anything in the meantime?"

"It's pretty quiet here, so we're focused on those drop-off kittens. Bekah and I can handle things until you get back."

When she'd accepted Erin's job offer, Heather hadn't anticipated inheriting such an accomplished staff. Yet another pleasant surprise in this picturesque town that she hadn't even heard of until a month ago. By the time she checked her few emails and responded to a thumbs-up text from Bailey's day care teacher, Josh emerged from his ordeal with a much thicker wrapping on his injured hand and a lollipop in the other.

"I was brave," he explained before popping the treat into his mouth.

"It's a good thing you're built sturdy," the doctor teased him with a chuckle. "'Cause you sure do take a beating on that farm."

As if on cue, a gust of wind banged several of the hinged wooden shutters against the side of the house. Before anyone could comment on the noise, a boom of thunder rattled the air, followed almost immediately by a flash of lightning.

Then a deafening crack split the air, unlike anything she'd ever heard in her life. Josh's eyes zoomed in on something outside, and he tossed away his lollipop as he ran from the lobby. "Doc, call the fire department!"

Following his line of sight, Heather saw what had propelled him to make such a dramatic exit. On the other side of the town square was the old Colonial that housed the day care Mrs. Sheppard was so excited about. The front section of the house had been crushed under an enormous oak tree, obviously felled by the lightning strike.

Bailey.

Stifling a horrified scream, Heather raced after Josh, only to be thrown back by a stiff wind driving a wall of rain so fierce, it nearly knocked her down. Struggling against the storm, she doggedly fought her way across the park, arriving at the building a few seconds after Josh.

The door to a side landing was open, and three women stood there, apparently trying to decide how to best get the children to safety. Dodging fallen limbs and a tangle of branches, Josh pushed toward the porch with Heather close on his heels. When they reached the house, she was terrified to see that the tree had only partially fallen, the rest of it hanging precariously by what appeared to be nothing more than a few splinters.

"Everyone okay?" he asked no one in particular, glancing at the roiling clouds overhead.

"I think so," one of the teachers said. "We're counting heads right now. We need to get out of here before the rest of that tree comes down on us."

"Good idea," he replied in a voice that Heather thought was abnormally calm considering the perilous situation. "How many kids are here today?"

"Ten, and they can all walk on their own."

"They'll fit in my truck. I'll be right back."

Heather gave him back his keys and begged him to hurry, but he was already dashing across the park. She stayed behind to help gather the children together, all the while searching the frightened group for Bailey. Just as Josh's truck pulled up alongside the landing, the fourth teacher joined them, a grim expression on her face.

"What's wrong?" Heather demanded, feeling panic starting to creep in. "Where's Bailey?"

"She went to the bathroom just before things got bad. I tried yelling in to her, but I couldn't hear anything over the wind. I didn't see her anywhere else, so I think she's still in there. I'm so sorry, but I couldn't get through to her. We'll have to wait for the fire crew."

The emergency siren in town began wailing as the young woman sent a look toward the front section of the house buried beneath the trunk of a tree at least six feet in diameter. Seized with dread, Heather took one step in that direction before a pair of strong hands clamped down on her shoulders to stop her.

Infuriated by the manhandling, she jerked free and glowered up at Josh. "What do you think you're doing?"

"Give these ladies a hand getting the kids over to the church," he replied in that calm, steady voice, cradling her trembling hand in his as he pressed his keys into her palm. "You'll all be safe there until the storm's over."

"I'm not leaving Bailey here. She could be hurt." *Or worse*, she added silently.

"I'll get her, and we'll meet you over there in a few minutes," he said as if they were discussing plans to rendezvous at the playground. When she refused to move, he gave her a gentle smile. "I promise."

Recognizing that she wouldn't be much help with the dangerous heavy lifting he'd have to do just to reach the bathrooms, Heather reluctantly gave in. "She hasn't met you, and she's been taught never to go anywhere with a stranger. Her safe word is *unicorn*. That little girl means everything to me," she added as tears slipped down her cheeks. "Please don't let anything happen to her."

"I won't."

With that simple vow, he was gone.

The restrooms were at the very front of the house, and Josh carefully picked his way through the rubble, moving as quickly as he dared. If he could safely slide an obstacle aside he did, but for the most part he was ducking and crawling. Built of century-old oak, the remaining trusses overhead didn't look like much to him, and the groaning timbers indicated that the structure wouldn't hold up much longer.

After what felt like forever, he found the door to the girls' bathroom lying askew on the floor, the painted picture of Little Bo-Peep torn from all but one of its screws. The jamb was cockeyed but more or less intact, and he murmured a quick prayer for Bailey's safety before stepping inside. The lights had been knocked from their sockets, so the only light came from a small window. Dust and debris hung in the air like a dense fog, making it nearly impossible for him to see.

Taking out his phone, he turned on its flashlight and swept the room, hunting for a child who was probably scared out of her mind. A huge limb had crushed the stalls, but thankfully no one was in either of them. The shrieking wind died down for a few seconds, and he heard a whimper off to his right. He swung the light around to find a dust-covered little girl cowering under one of the sinks.

"Hey there," he said in a purposefully casual tone. "I'm thinking you must be Bailey Fitzgerald."

Blue eyes wide with fear, she mutely stared back at him. She was holding her left arm but otherwise appeared to be unharmed. The roof shifted ominously overhead, and he realized that if he didn't get her out of here quickly, they might be trapped inside when the rafters caved in. He didn't dare crawl over to her, for fear of disturbing the pile of debris that was currently holding up what remained of the ceiling.

Since she was much smaller than him, he thought Bailey could wiggle out of her hiding place and over to where he was standing without compromising the stack. Hoping to coax her into the open, he forced a grin. "I'm Josh Kinley, Erin's little brother. Your aunt sent me in here to make sure you washed your hands."

That got him nothing, and panic started creeping up his spine. If she wouldn't come to him, he'd have to go in after her and risk toppling the pile onto them both. Just when he was beginning to think that was his only option, he remembered what Heather had told him about unicorns. He didn't know what a safe word was, but he figured he had nothing to lose by trying.

"Your aunt said that when I found you, I should tell you 'unicorn.'"

Like a key to a lock, the single word opened her up, and in a trembling voice she said, "I'm scared."

"I know, but you're gonna be fine. If I hold this beam up, do you think you can crawl over here?"

She nodded, and he braced his hands on the timber to keep it steady while she shimmied across the floor. When she reached him, he let the beam go and swept her into his arms, backing into the hallway as quickly as he could. Several chunks of ceiling rained down on them, and she shrank against him with a fearful scream. Hunching around her to protect her as much as he could, he hurried from the collapsing building, maneuvering around upended furniture and sections of the roof that were hailing down on him at an alarming rate.

Each chunk was larger and heavier than the last, and by the time he burst from the side door, every inch of him felt as if it had been bruised in a fight. But Bailey was in one piece, and that was all that mattered. Josh didn't stop to check her over but ran straight to the church, where an anxious Heather was waiting just inside the entryway doors, her worried gaze fixed on the ruined day care center.

When she saw them coming, she bolted down the front steps and into the driving rain. She met them in the middle of Main Street, oblivious to the storm still raging around her. Without a word, Josh handed Bailey over to her, watching as they hugged and cried in a touching reunion that might have ended so differently.

"My arm hurts," Bailey said as they made their way up the steps to where it was warm and dry. It struck Josh that the small white chapel was serving as a sanctuary for all of them, and he looked up with a grateful smile. He was too exhausted to do more than that, but he was sure that God knew what he meant.

"Doc Sheppard can take care of that," Josh assured her, nodding to where the kind man was tending to one of her classmates. "And if you're brave, he'll give you your choice of lollipops."

"I like grape."

"Yeah? Me, too." Grinning at the resilient child, he shifted his gaze to Heather, whose face was beginning to regain some of its color. "How 'bout you?"

It was obvious she was still trying to shake off their ordeal, though she looked up as if thinking it over. "I like cherry."

"I'll ask the doctor to give you a cherry one, Aunt Heather," Bailey suggested. "You were brave today, too."

"Thanks, bean. I appreciate that." Wrapping her in a hug, Heather looked up at Josh with tears of gratitude shining in her eyes. "I know it's not close to being enough for what you did, but thank you."

"Aw, it was nothin'," he replied, ticking Bailey's nose with his finger. "Always glad to lend a lady a hand."

"You're a hero," the girl informed him. "Like Superman."

"Well, now, that's kinda cool."

"Yes, it is," Heather agreed, "but right now, I think we should get you both taken care of."

"I'm fine," Josh assured her. When she nodded at his left hand, he looked down to see that the nice, neat wrapping was now filthy and shredded into several pieces. "Huh. How 'bout that?"

Tired and half-drowned, the three of them crossed the church to where Doc Sheppard was using one of the front pews as a makeshift office. He gave Josh a proud smile, then turned his attention to Bailey. "And what brings you by to see me, young lady?"

"My arm hurts. And I like grape lollipops."

"I see you've been talking to Josh." The grandfatherly man chuckled as he examined her arm. "He's one of my best customers, you know."

While he chatted with Bailey and assessed her injuries, Heather glanced over at Josh and gave him a sweet smile that warmed him from his dripping hair to his waterlogged boots. He didn't want to ruin one of the antique oak pews, so he braced his back against the wall and slid down to sit on the carpet runner that stretched the length of the side aisle to wait for his turn with the doctor.

What a day, he mused, taking advantage of the relative calm to close his eyes. Right now, that plan of watching TV that Doc had mentioned was sounding pretty good to him.

Chapter Four

Heather wasn't sure what to do next.

The kindly doctor had cleaned and inspected Bailey's elbow, then checked her over and pronounced her slightly bruised but ready to go. With a grape lollipop tucked in her mouth, Bailey seemed none the worse for wear as they followed Josh out to his pickup, which the day care class was calling the Rescue Truck.

Heather's nerves were another story altogether.

She'd never been so terrified in her life, and when she reached out to tousle her niece's hair for the third time, Bailey pulled away as she buckled her seat belt.

"I'm fine, Aunt Heather," she announced in an overly patient tone that betrayed her annoyance. "You can stop smushing me."

"Sorry. I guess I'm not good in a crisis."

"Seriously?" Josh teased with a sidelong grin at her. "You're a vet."

"Human crisis," she clarified, frowning back. "I can't believe you're being so blasé about this. If it weren't for you..." She trailed off, unable to complete the thought. If she was being honest, she had to acknowledge that she hadn't yet accepted her brother's sudden death, and she was still learning to navigate her responsibilities as a guardian. If anything happened to Bailey, she'd never forgive herself.

The twinkle in his blue eyes dimmed a bit, chasing away the smile. "My turn to apologize. You might not wanna hear this, but I know how you feel."

Her favorite phrase, she thought bitterly. She'd heard it so many times at the funeral, she'd barely managed not to scream at the well-meaning guests. Smothering that same impulse now, she summoned the tone she'd cultivated for chauvinistic professors who'd dared to question her choice of career. "About what?"

"Your brother," he replied quietly, staring out the windshield as he pulled onto Main Street. "We lost my dad in a car accident a few years ago. It changes your perspective on things."

She gave him a long look, but he didn't meet her eyes. When she realized that was his in-tent, she decided it was probably best for both of them. After the scare she'd had, seeing sympathy in the eyes of this selfless, courageous man might just make her cry. She was fairly certain that was the last thing either of them wanted. "Yes, it does. Thank you for understanding."

He nodded, then angled a glance down at Bailey. "How's your arm feeling?"

"Okay. Can I turn on the radio?"

"Sure, sweetness. Pick whatever you want."

"Sweetness?" she echoed, grinning up at him. "That's a nice nickname."

"Then it's yours. You were pretty awesome today, so I'm thinking you should get whatever you want."

She cast a woeful look through the rain-streaked window at the park. The powerful storm had moved on, but not before dropping several enormous limbs on top of what had been a sprawling wooden playground only a few hours ago. "Mr. Kinley, do you think someone can fix that?"

He hesitated, and Heather guessed that he was trying to come up with a way to be truthful but encouraging. Most adults would've patted Bailey on the head and told her not to worry about it, but not Josh. He was treating her with the same respect he'd shown Heather, and she appreciated his generous attitude toward her niece. She didn't know him well, but she couldn't deny that there was a lot to like about this tall, easygoing country boy.

"I'd imagine so," he finally replied, "but not for a while. It'll take some serious cash and a lot of hours no one has to spare this time of year."

Bailey sighed. "I saw a bunch of kids playing over there yesterday. It looked like they were having a lot of fun."

Josh's eyes flicked toward Heather, but she had no idea what he was after, so she kept quiet, waiting to hear what he'd say next.

"Tell you what," he said as he stopped for an elderly couple in the crosswalk. "I'll start pulling a crew together to make the repairs on one condition."

"What?" Bailey asked eagerly.

"You and your aunt have to help raise the money we'll need to replace the materials."

"I don't know, Josh," Heather said instinctively. "With my new job, I'm going to be awfully busy."

"And I'm just a kid," Bailey added. "What can I do?"

"Folks need a good reason to donate money to the project. Who better to ask them than a girl who's going to enjoy the end result?"

"What if they say no?" she asked.

"Then you ask someone else," he replied with a chuckle. "That's how the Oaks Crossing Rescue Center operates all year long, and they're doing it well enough to bring your aunt here, aren't they?"

"I guess." Hope shone in Bailey's china-blue eyes that were so much like Craig's as she looked at Heather. "Is it okay?"

After the day the little girl had endured, how could she possibly say no? Besides, Josh was in the middle of planting season, and he'd volunteered time he clearly didn't have to spare. It wasn't as if she could claim to be busier than he was. "Of course it is. Maybe some of the kids in your class will help, too. Then you'll be raising money and making friends at the same time."

Josh flashed her a grin of approval that went a long way toward soothing her frazzled nerves. Her last boyfriend had broken things off when Bailey moved in with her, claiming he didn't have the energy for a child during his residency. Heather had decided that she and Bailey would be better off not relying on someone else who'd leave when things didn't go his way.

Since Heather was independent by nature, it didn't bother her all that much when people disapproved of her choices. Being a woman in a traditionally male field had made her even more adamant about following her own path. But she had to admit, it was comforting to be around someone who seemed to be on the same page she was.

Josh kept up pleasant conversation with Bailey until they reached the curb outside Pampered Paws. The respite gave Heather a chance to regain her composure, and she realized she had a problem. Clearly, Bailey should be home resting, but their apartment was still a disorganized jumble of boxes and furniture—not the best place for a child who'd been through such a harrowing ordeal.

Their only option was the clinic, which didn't seem like a better choice to her. Heather was used to dropping Bailey at day care and then pushing from one end of the day to the other until her work was done. In the month she'd been a full-time parent, she'd never had to cope with anything other than a healthy child. This was completely new territory for her, and she was beginning to understand the dilemma working mothers faced every day when their children's well-being was at stake.

Before she could say anything, Josh stepped in. "So, all this rain washed out what I had planned for today. If you ladies would like a little help getting Bailey's room set up, I'm available."

It was as if he'd read her mind, and Heather felt a combination of awe and relief. Even though he was single, clearly he was familiar with kids and how important their treasures were to making them feel comfortable. While he could have benefitted from some rest himself, she was more grateful for his offer than she'd been for anything in a long time.

"What do you think, Bailey?" she asked in a light voice. "Should we let a boy into our clubhouse?"

Her niece gave him a quick once-over and grinned. "I guess he's okay. But you have to do whatever we say, even if you don't like it."

"Aw, man, you sound just like my big sister," he grumbled, even though his eyes twinkled in fun. "She loves ordering me and my brothers around."

"Hey, that's my boss you're talking about," Heather reminded him with a laugh. "I think Erin's wonderful, so you'd better watch what you say about her when I'm around."

"Yes, ma'am." When she reached out to open her door, he stopped her with a hand on her shoulder. "I'll get it."

"Really, I can—"

"I know you can," he said with yet another warm grin. "But us Southern boys open doors for ladies. Just go with it."

She opened her mouth to argue further, until she caught Bailey staring up at him with a hero-worshipping look on her face. She could assert her independence later, Heather decided. For now, she'd humor him and play along. "Okay, then. Thank you."

"Anytime."

Inside, they didn't get more than a couple of feet before Erin Stewart hurried over to intercept them near the door. "The whole town's in a tizzy about what happened at the preschool. Are you guys okay?"

"Never better," Josh assured her in a casual tone. "Why?"

"Oh, you." She smacked him in the shoulder, frowning when he winced. "When I called earlier, you said you were fine."

"He's a hero, Erin," Bailey chimed in, going on to relate the whole incident with wide, shining eyes. By the time she was finished, the tall country boy sounded like a knight in faded denim. And quite honestly, Heather didn't mind admitting that she heartily agreed with her niece.

A soft mewling sound caught Bailey's attention, and she ran over to the padded display area in the front bay window. Bracing her hands on the Plexiglas enclosure, she sighed. "These are the cutest kittens ever. Where did they come from?"

"Someone dropped them off at the rescue center a few weeks ago." Erin joined her, smiling down at the wriggling mass of paws and legs. "They're big enough for people to adopt now, so I brought them in here. We usually find homes for them in a couple of days."

"That's 'cause they're so cute," Bailey cooed, gently petting one between the ears.

The batch of furry darlings reminded Heather of the litter that had come in on her first day at the clinic. "Do you know how the new ones are doing?"

"I talked to Sierra about half an hour ago, and she said the larger ones are responding well." Glancing over at Bailey, Erin leaned in and murmured, "She's afraid the tiny one's not going to make it. She's still dehydrated and sluggish, no matter what she and Bekah do."

That was completely unacceptable. This was her first week on the job, and Heather wasn't about to lose a patient if there was anything she could do to avoid it.

Then a small voice in the back of her mind whispered *Bailey needs you, too.*

A few months ago, that wouldn't have been a consideration for Heather, and she'd have dashed into the clinic to make sure she was doing everything humanly possible to save the failing kitten. But now, she had someone else to care for, and the decision wasn't as easy as it once would have been.

"Aunt Heather?"

Dragged from her tangled thoughts, she focused on Bailey. "Yes?"

"Is something wrong? You look sad."

Her instinct was to reassure the little girl gazing up at her with worry clouding her eyes. Then she recalled how Josh had handled a difficult question from her earlier and opted for the truth. "There's a sick kitten at the clinic, and I'm trying to figure out how to give the vet tech instructions for taking care of her."

Bailey's disheveled ponytail bobbed as she cocked her head in confusion. "Why aren't you going to do it yourself?"

"I'm staying here with you, silly bean," Heather replied, hugging her lightly. "You've had kind of a tough day."

"But that kitten needs you."

"So do you."

After a few moments, that precious little face brightened. "I could come with you. That way, you can take care of us both."

"I don't know," she hedged, glancing at Erin for some kind of direction. "Kids don't usually go to work like that."

"It's not a problem," Erin assured her, winking at Bailey. "We'll call it Take Your Niece to Work Day."

Her boss was being so understanding, Heather couldn't quite believe it. During her last assignment, her new status as Bailey's parent had caused her no end of problems at work. It seemed that for the Kinleys, family came first. What a refreshing change. After agreeing to the arrangement, she realized something. "My car's at the clinic."

"Mine's not," Josh reminded her with a broad grin. "I'm going out there, anyway."

"Do you just go around town looking for damsels in distress?"

The teasing was very unlike her, and Heather felt her cheeks reddening in embarrassment. Fortunately, he either didn't notice or was so accustomed to making women blush that it didn't faze him.

"Not hardly," he replied easily as he strolled over to open the door. "But I don't leave 'em standing in the road, either. Shall we?"

"Yes," Bailey answered for them both, hurrying out of the store. "That little baby needs our help."

"I guess we're going now," Heather told Erin with a laugh. "I'll check in with you later."

"Sounds good. By the way, that lease you signed allows pets, in case you were wondering."

"We're not adopting any."

"Keep telling yourself that," Erin said with a knowing smile. "I'll be praying for that poor little thing. I've got a soft spot for lost critters."

"And they're all better off for it," Josh commented proudly.

"Get out before I put you to work, Kinley boy," she shot back with a fond smile.

He took the ribbing in stride, grinning back before motioning Heather out the door in front of him. The gallant gesture seemed at odds with his shredded jeans and battered work boots, but somehow it worked for him. Between the country boy clothes and those warm blue eyes and strong build, there was a lot about Josh Kinley for a girl to admire.

Not that she should be thinking of him as anything other than her boss's brother, she reminded herself sternly. Josh had made it clear that he adored his hometown, but Heather would go bonkers spending the rest of her life in such a quiet place. Impossible as it might seem to someone else, she already missed the excitement of living in a large city. She had fond memories of everything from cute boutiques to the endless array of restaurants and entertainment that could be found everywhere you looked.

Heather had chosen to relocate to this sleepy town because she believed it would be a good environment for Bailey, and she'd simply have to make the best of it. As she went out to his truck, she knew that recognizing those very fundamental differences between Josh and her should have made her feel more confident about remaining strictly friends with the engaging farmer.

Instead, it made her wonder if she and Bailey would be missing out on something. What exactly, she wasn't sure, but she couldn't shake the feeling that if she decided to take that detour, it just might be worth the risk.

It didn't look good to him.

Josh stood in the doorway of the exam room, frustrated that there was nothing he could do for the sick kitten. He marveled at the way Heather went about her business, thorough but gentle while she assessed the tiny cat's condition. She cradled the filthy ball of fur against her chest, heedless of the grime left behind on her pretty blouse.

The pathetic little thing opened its mouth

in a meek attempt to cry, but she was so weak that nothing came out. Josh had a soft heart, and it was killing him to watch the helpless animal suffer this way. He couldn't imagine how it would be to do this job, day after day, knowing full well that some you could save and some you couldn't. He didn't know how Heather did it, and his respect for the empathetic young vet rose several notches.

"That's a girl," she cooed, gently dabbing disinfectant over eyes that were sealed shut by what seemed to be an infection. "These are looking better already."

Josh wasn't convinced of that, but he opted not to say so. When Bailey crept in for a closer look, he was glad he'd kept his opinion to himself.

"What a sweetie pie. Can I hold her?"

Heather hesitated, for obvious reasons. With everything Bailey had been through, he could easily understand why her aunt wouldn't want to risk her getting attached to something else she could lose. But then, she surprised him. "That's a good idea. You can keep her warm while I get some more medicine for her."

Once the kitten was settled in Bailey's arms, the shy smile he'd seen earlier blossomed into one that would rival a sunny summer day.

"Don't worry, baby. We're going to take good care of you, and you'll be good as new."

Josh could see that Heather didn't share her niece's optimism, but to her credit she kept up a positive front. "Absolutely. We Fitzgeralds don't give up that easily."

She went over to a tall cabinet and stood on tiptoe to reach something on the highest shelf. Finally seeing a way he could be useful, Josh stepped in to help.

"What do you need?" She rattled off a word that sounded like Greek to him, and he chuckled. "What color is it?"

"Light green."

He plucked it off the shelf and handed it to her, and she thanked him with a wan smile. "I hope this does the trick."

"Can't hurt to try, right?" When she shook her head, he took the opening to bolster her spirits. "You've had a killer day, and you've handled it like a champ. No reason for that to change now."

A slow, dawning smile worked its way across her features, and the cool blue eyes warmed with gratitude. "Thank you, Josh. That's sweet of you to say."

"Sweet, nothin'. Erin's as tough as they come, and she thinks you're perfect for this job. From what I've seen, she's right. Again," he added with a mock groan.

"Does that happen often?" Heather asked while she mixed a foul-smelling concoction for her patient.

"Yeah, but don't tell her I said so. She'll never let me live it down."

"My lips are sealed." She ripped open a packet of sugar substitute and added a dab of it to the medicine, stirring it in before pulling a dose into the smallest eyedropper he'd ever seen. Holding it within the kitten's reach, she dabbed a drop onto the withered lips. "Come on, now. Just a little."

Most of it went down the cat's chin, but she managed to swallow enough to satisfy her doctor. After coaxing her to drink some formula, Heather stood back and folded her arms in a thoughtful pose. "That's all we can do for now. In about an hour, Sierra will be able to see if it helped."

The scrap of fur rested her head on Bailey's chest and let out a pitiful whimper before falling into an exhausted sleep. Cuddling her close, the girl dropped a kiss between her ears. "Sweet dreams, little baby."

Bailey leaned down to put the kitten back into its blanket-lined box, but the motion woke her up and she let out a strangled, desperate cry that would have gotten sympathy from even the most dedicated cat hater.

"We have to stay here with her, Aunt Heather," the girl announced firmly, quickly scooping up her new friend. "She needs me."

Heather glanced at him, but Josh knew it wasn't his place to interfere and kept his expression as neutral as he could manage. This perplexing woman and her adorable niece had started getting to him already, and he didn't trust himself to do anything more than maintain his helpful attitude. His impulsive heart had been shattered when the girl he'd loved more than anything had refused a future with him and walked out of his life, and he wasn't eager to go through that again.

After Cindy left him with his pride in tatters, he'd been careful to keep his head around women. If he put that aside and got involved in the Fitzgeralds' family business, he wasn't sure he'd be able to back away from them afterward.

"You know this is my job." Hunkering down to the girl's level, Heather stroked Bailey's hair in a maternal gesture. "I love animals very much, and I do all I can to make them better. But we can't adopt every sick kitten that comes in here."

"Not every one. *This* one."

Bailey rubbed cheeks with the pitiful stray, and Josh could sense Heather's professional demeanor wavering in the face of her niece's plea. Finally, the tension left her face, replaced by an indulgent smile.

"Okay," she finally agreed, "but it's a big responsibility taking care of a sick animal. And I'm going to be honest with you—no matter what we do, she might not make it. Are you sure you're ready for that?"

Eyes large and way too serious for a five-year-old, Bailey nodded somberly. "I understand."

"All right, then," Heather said as she stood. "First things first. She needs a name."

"Annabelle."

"That was fast," Josh teased with a chuckle. "How'd you come up with that?"

"Easy," Bailey replied airily. "She looks like an Annabelle."

"Well, you know that once you name 'em, they own you." Angling a look over at Heather, he was pleased to hear her laugh.

"Is that right? Isn't it the other way around?"

"I guess you'll find out."

"Yes," she agreed, giving him a heartwarming smile. "I guess we will."

Chapter Five

❦

She'd never been more grateful to whoever had discovered the energizing benefits of coffee.

After a long night of watching over Bailey and tending to Annabelle, when Friday morning rolled around, Heather was exhausted. A steamy hot shower hadn't helped very much, but now that she was bringing in some caffeine, she could feel her brain starting to wake up one synapse at a time. It was hardly the gourmet coffee she'd been so fond of in Detroit, but it was doing the job, and right now that was good enough.

She idly picked up her charging cell phone and glanced at a text from Tammy Sheppard that had come in while she was getting ready.

Hope Bailey is feeling better. Day care will be housed in church basement rooms until further notice. Looking forward to seeing both of you again soon.

Overall, Bailey had held up yesterday like a trouper, but once they'd gotten home and cued up her favorite movie, she'd crashed on the couch with Annabelle snoozing contentedly in her arms. Even picking her up and moving her to her room hadn't wakened her, so Heather thought the best course was to let the exhausted child sleep as long as she wanted and then go from there.

After checking the time, she knew that someone would be at the clinic for early animal care by now. When she dialed the main number, Bekah answered on the first ring.

"Good morning," she all but sang. "How are you and your girl doing today?"

"Everything's quiet so far. I hate to do this to you my first week, but I might not be at the clinic until later, if at all."

"Don't even think about it. Family comes first, and Bailey needs you. How's our furry little patient doing?"

"Stable," Heather replied around a yawn. "I was up every four hours with her, but she's been holding her own. How are the others?"

"Listen for yourself."

A chorus of demanding mewls drifted over

the line, and Heather smiled. "They sound healthy enough."

"And hungry. There's nothing going on here that Sierra and I can't manage, so don't worry. If we need you, we know how to reach you."

"If there are any emergencies, consider me on call."

"Will do. Have a good day, and give Bailey a hug from us."

Touched by the young mother-to-be's thoughtfulness, Heather thanked her then hung up and set her phone down on the breakfast bar. She was accustomed to being on the lowest rung of the ladder, and this was the first time she'd taken a day off from work for anything other than a debilitating bout of pneumonia she'd developed one frigid winter. But she was a parent now, she reminded herself. The staff at the Oaks Crossing Rescue Center seemed to be on board with what that kind of commitment entailed, but when she negotiated with future employers, she'd have to make sure to clearly address personal time in any long-term arrangement.

Her life had changed, and while she was still getting used to what that meant, she was savvy enough to realize that there would be times when Bailey's needs would trump everything else.

Moving as quietly as she could, she took advantage of her unexpected free time to finish loading their kitchenware into the cupboards and drawers. She was almost done when she heard the padding of bare feet in the hallway.

Looking up from where she was sliding pots and pans onto a shelf, she smiled at the sight of her tousled niece carefully holding her new friend. "Good morning, bean. Did you sleep well?"

"Mmm-hmm." She lifted the kitten and rubbed cheeks with her. "Annabelle did, too. She keeps squeaking, though, so I think she's hungry."

"I've got formula in the fridge, all ready to go. How 'bout you? I'm sure that sugar crunch cereal you like is around here somewhere."

"Okay."

Bailey clambered up on one of the bar stools at the breakfast bar and set Annabelle down on the other. The kitten blinked her rheumy eyes in confusion, but her ears perked up when Heather walked around the counter with a cup of warm formula and a dropper. More of the food went down her throat this time, a sign that the tiny cat was gaining some desperately needed strength. The two girls finished their meal at the same time, and Heather counted the morning as a success.

Simple pleasures, she thought. They really were the most precious.

Then, to her surprise, Bailey asked, "Are they having day care today?"

"Yes, at the church. Miss Tammy texted to let us know they're going to be meeting there until the house is fixed." Gazing down at her plucky niece, she went on. "I wasn't sure you'd want to go, so I called work and told them I'd be staying here with you. It's your call, though."

"The teachers are fun, and everyone's really nice," Bailey explained. "My friend Cara started this week, too, so if I don't go, she'll be the only new kid in the class. She's kind of shy, and I don't want her to be lonely."

Heather's heart swelled with emotion, and she felt tears of pride stinging her eyes. After all she'd endured since her father's death, Bailey's sympathy for her timid classmate was incredible.

Putting aside emotions that would only upset her brave girl, Heather gave her a quick hug. "You're a very good friend to Cara, and I'm sure everyone else will be happy to see you, too. Why don't you go get ready, and Annabelle and I will drop you off at the church on our way to the clinic. She can rest in my office when I'm working, and I'll make sure she gets her food and medicine during the day."

"Maybe she'll be strong enough to play with her brothers and sisters soon," Bailey suggested hopefully, then went into her room to get dressed. A quick braiding and teeth brushing later, the three of them went down the stairs and into the pet store, which had just opened for business.

There, of all people, stood Josh Kinley.

"Mornin', ladies," he drawled, one cheek dimpling as he grinned. "How's everyone doing today?"

"Great!" Bailey replied, all but skipping over to join Erin and him near the cash register and holding up her charge. "Annabelle's eyes are much better. See? They're blue, just like mine and Aunt Heather's."

Very carefully, he took the kitten from her. Big as he was, Heather marveled at how gently he handled the tiny creature. "They sure are. I didn't know she was so many different colors."

"We gave her a bath when we got home last night," Bailey informed him proudly. "She's much fluffier now."

Handing her back, Josh said, "I don't know, sweetness. She looks like trouble to me."

He added a mischievous grin, then angled a look over at Heather that made her heart stutter in a way that was exciting and alarming all at the same time. She'd received that kind of glance from men more times than she cared to count, but none of them had ever affected her like this. Apparently, there was something different about the tall country boy with the warm eyes and quick smile. Maybe it was his caring nature, or the way he spoke so respectfully to Bailey, rather than dismissing her as a child.

Or maybe it was something else completely. But right now Heather didn't have the energy to ponder anything beyond how to get through the day and fall into bed at the end of it. So she switched tracks to something that would be safer than flirting with the very charming Josh Kinley. "It's nice to see you again. The weather's so good today, I assumed you'd be busy at the farm getting caught up on your plowing. What brings you into town?"

In answer, he tapped the top of what appeared to be an oversize condiment jar. "I picked this up from Cam. Erin's gonna set it on the counter here to collect donations from her customers to rebuild the playground."

Erin rolled her eyes. "And I just finished telling him that we need something nicer than this. He and Cam think all we have to do is cut a hole in the top and slap a sign on the front, and folks will drop their money in."

"Is that safe?" Heather asked, stunned by what they had in mind. "I mean, won't people just reach in and help themselves to whatever's inside when you're not at the counter?"

"Steal money from a bunch of kids?" Josh scoffed. "Are you serious?"

"Where I'm from, a shop owner wouldn't even think of leaving cash out in the open and unguarded like that."

There was that dimple again. "Then I guess it's a good thing you and Bailey landed here."

She couldn't agree more, but there was no way she was sharing that with someone she'd just met. Besides, she didn't want him to mistake their conversation for flirting.

"Anyway," Erin interrupted, "when you guys came in, we were debating how to decorate this ugly thing to make it more presentable. Any ideas?"

"Marketing is hardly my strong point," Heather replied. "But I understand Bekah does your website, and it's fabulous. I'm sure she'd have some suggestions for you."

Erin considered that for a moment, then wrinkled her nose and looked down at Bailey. "Bekah's got a lot going on right now, being pregnant and all. Besides, I think someone younger would be better suited to this sort of job. Do you have any ideas about what we should do?"

To Heather's astonishment, her niece jumped right in. "The castle and pirate ship were so nice before. Maybe you could show people a picture of how they used to look and one of them now."

"Awesome," Josh approved with the kind of enthusiasm Heather had seldom observed in an adult. Beneath all that tanned muscle ran a fun-loving streak unlike any she'd seen in other men she'd met, and she couldn't help wondering if he approached everything in his life that way. If he did, she had to admit that she was more than a little envious of his bright attitude. She was fairly serious by nature, but perhaps she could learn to be more upbeat.

Going along with his positive response, she gently tugged Bailey's braid. "Tell you what. After I drop you at day care, I'll go by the park and take some pictures of the playground. I'm sure Erin can find us some of how it looked before, and we'll ask Cam to give us some more of these big empty jars. Then tonight you and I can design the signs, print them out and glue them on the containers. Tomorrow's Saturday, so we can go around town and leave them at businesses where people are sure to notice them when they're out shopping."

"I'll get a list of stores that'll let you drop them off," Erin offered. "I can't imagine anyone would mind, though, since it's their kids and grandkids who have so much fun playing over there at the park."

The speediness of the town's reaction to the storm was impressive. Heather laughed. "Do people around here solve all their problems this fast?"

"When there's something to be done, everyone pitches in," Josh informed her as he strolled toward the door. "That's the beauty of living in a place like Oaks Crossing."

So she was learning, Heather mused as she and Bailey followed him outside. This was precisely why she'd chosen to move them to this sleepy Bluegrass town. The peaceful surroundings here would give them both a chance to get their feet under them and adjust to being together.

And then? She wasn't sure, but she'd figure it out when the time came. Bailey would be dependent on her for years to come, and Heather had every intention of living up to her niece's expectations. After worrying about only herself for so long, Craig's death had changed everything for her.

Now—and far into the future—Bailey was

the absolute center of her world. Everything else would just have to wait.

The middle Kinley brother, Drew, let out a low whistle. "This is a mess."

He and Josh, along with oldest brother, Mike, were standing in the town park, just outside the barricade of sawhorses that outlined the wrecked playground in yellow tape marked SHERIFF'S LINE—DO NOT CROSS. Just in case anyone misunderstood the potential danger of venturing inside the boundary, every few feet there was a sign that warned of the dire consequences to anyone stupid enough to believe that the order didn't apply to them. While Josh doubted their laid-back sheriff would actually toss someone in jail for slipping past the barrier, he was pretty sure that the fine mentioned on the signs would be enforced.

"Abby's heartbroken over this," Mike commented sadly. "She loves playing here with her friends after church."

"Yeah, Erin said Parker's pretty bummed, too," Drew added. "The adoption's official now, but I guess he still has a hard time making friends. Over here he could feel like one of the crew instead of a kid trying to recover from a tough background."

Their discussion reminded Josh of Bailey wishing that she'd been able to experience the playground before it was destroyed. "Summer vacation's coming up pretty quick. We need to get this place squared away or the kids'll drive their parents and babysitters totally nuts looking for stuff to do."

"What've you got in mind?" Mike asked, eyeing him with something that looked an awful lot like respect. Coming from the big brother he admired so much, it meant a lot to him.

"Erin's already started fund-raising, and Bailey will be helping her out. I promised her I'd pull a crew together to get the damaged sections put back together."

Knowing full well that they'd tease him mercilessly, he didn't dare mention Heather's name. But these two had known him his entire life. He didn't have to say it for them to hear it.

"Bailey, huh?" Mike chuckled. "She's five years old, right?"

"So?"

Drew draped an arm around Mike's shoulders. "So we're thinking she's probably gonna have some help from her aunt. Her very pretty aunt."

"Grow up," Josh growled. "It's not like that with Heather and me."

"Why not?" Drew asked, grinning at him like an idiot.

Aggravated by the detour their conversation had taken from let's-all-work-together to let's-pick-on-Josh, he glared back but stubbornly refused to answer.

"I'm thinking you got warned," Mike jumped in. "Seeing as Drew and I are married now, you're the only one of us left to cause trouble with the ladies. What'd Erin say to you?"

They had him dead to rights, so as much as he hated to back down, Josh figured he'd be wasting his breath if he continued stonewalling them. "That Heather's strictly off-limits. The princess said the clinic needs a permanent vet more than I need another girlfriend."

"She's got a point there," Drew commented, rubbing his chin. "You go through 'em pretty quick."

Josh snorted. "Like you two were any better. I learned everything I know about women from you." When they both grinned, he shook his head in defeat. He'd spent his whole life trying to best them at something—anything— but apparently his winless streak wasn't going to end today. "Anyway, Erin doesn't want to risk setting up a situation that might turn bad and make Heather want to leave."

Like Cindy had, he added silently. He could

still see her, staring at him with tears in her eyes while she slowly shook her head and handed back the ring he'd saved for months to buy her. She loved him, but there was a big world out there, and she didn't want to settle down until she'd explored some of it. For months afterward, he'd mooned over her, waiting for his sweet country girl to come back and tell him she'd made a mistake. But she never did.

So, like countless guys before him, he'd dusted himself off and gotten on with his life. He was a Kinley boy, after all, and there were plenty of women around for him to spend his time with. The problem was, none of them gave him the same breathless feeling he'd gotten when he was with Cindy.

Until a few days ago when he stumbled across a feisty blonde pixie with a stern manner and a soft heart. Different from Cindy in just about every way, Heather fascinated him in a way he didn't quite understand.

"The word you're looking for is *smitten*," Mike suggested with a knowing smirk.

"What?"

"You're a lot of things," Drew explained, "but subtle ain't one of 'em. Anyone with eyes and half a working brain can see Heather's getting under your skin."

"You're outta your mind. I like her, and she likes me, the same way Bailey does. That's all."

His brothers traded a glance, but they didn't say anything more on the subject. Josh couldn't figure out why the ribbing had stopped so abruptly until he noticed them staring past him toward the other side of the park. He turned to find the lady they'd just been discussing taking the pictures she'd mentioned earlier. When she saw them, she waved and began picking her way through the grass and shattered bits of wood, frowning at the wrecked play structure.

When Heather reached them, she sighed. "It didn't look this bad to me the other day."

"You probably didn't notice, since you were so focused on your niece," Mike said, flashing Josh a prodding look.

"Oh, sorry," he stammered, feeling like a moron. "Heather Fitzgerald, this is my big brother, Mike, and my doofus brother, Drew."

Laughing, she shook hands with them. "I've met Bekah at the center, Drew, and she talks about you nonstop. I'm looking forward to meeting Lily sometime soon."

"My wife's always either at school or the farm," Mike said. "She and my daughter, Abby, hike over to the center whenever they can, so you're likely to run into them there eventually."

"Or you and Bailey could come to lunch on Sunday, meet the whole family."

Josh couldn't believe it was his own voice he heard. But he'd blurted out the invitation, and he couldn't take it back now, so he did his best to act cool about it.

The grateful smile she gave him made him glad he'd spoken up. "Thank you, Josh, that's very generous of you. We'd love to do that." Turning to Mike, she added, "I'd also love to meet some of the horses you've got. I haven't had a lot of experience with large animals, and it would be great to learn from someone who works with them every day."

"Happy to help."

Turning her attention back to Josh, she asked, "So, is this the construction crew you promised us?"

"The start of it, anyway. We were just saying how much the kids would miss playing here over summer vacation."

"Then I guess we'd better get it back into shape ASAP. See you Sunday." With a quick wave, she headed across the street to where her car was parked. After she'd driven away, Josh felt a familiar arm settle across his shoulders.

"Like I said, little brother," Drew gloated, "she's under your skin. You might as well just accept it."

For once, Josh didn't disagree with him. But he couldn't pursue Heather without risking bodily injury from Erin, so he decided it was best to put the fascinating veterinarian out of his mind. "So, we're obviously gonna need more hands to tackle such a big job. Got any suggestions?"

They put together a list of friends they thought might be willing to pitch in and then went their separate ways. As Josh drove back to the farm, he found himself thankful that he had so much plowing to catch up on. It would keep him on the tractor and well occupied for the rest of the week.

Until Sunday, anyway. By then, he'd have to come up with a way to keep Heather Fitzgerald at a nice, respectable distance. It was a stretch for him, trying to hold a beautiful woman at bay, but he didn't have a choice.

Even if Erin hadn't declared her off-limits, Josh had the nagging feeling that if he let himself get too close to the spunky city girl, he really would be in trouble.

The Sunday lunch that Josh had invited them to was quite the experience. Heather had never seen so many relatives all in one place outside of a full-blown Fitzgerald reunion.

Her own extended family was scattered

across the United States, and some even lived in Ireland, where her parents were currently doing a tour to reconnect with their roots. In contrast, the Kinleys had all stayed close to where they'd grown up, and from the bits of family news that she was able to pick up, most of their parents' many siblings had done the same. These days that was unusual, but Heather also thought it was wonderful. Close-knit and firmly grounded by the farm they were so devoted to keeping, the large, raucous family was nothing like the much smaller one she'd grown up in. And she loved it.

"Charlie, down," Josh's niece Abby firmly told an enormous golden retriever, who immediately removed his front paws from Bailey's waist and sat in front of her, swishing his feathery tail over the well-worn plank floor in the enormous kitchen. To Bailey, she said, "He gets excited meeting new people, but he wouldn't hurt you. He's just saying hello."

Bailey's hesitant look gave way to a bright smile as the dog extended his paw for her to shake. "Hello, Charlie. Nice to meet you."

He woofed quietly and looked over his shoulder at a graying Jack Russell who'd followed him in from the living room. His slow, stiff gait alerted Heather to the fact that he was arthritic, so she knelt on the floor to get on his level.

"This must be Sarge," she commented. "I've heard a lot of good things about you from Erin."

The terrier's eyes were cloudy with cataracts, and he sniffed at her in a curious manner that told her he didn't see as well as he once did. But he politely offered a paw, and she shook it gently to avoid hurting him.

"He's really old," Erin's son, Parker, informed her. "But he's a good friend for a young dog to have, 'cause he can teach Charlie how to behave. That just makes us love Sarge even more."

The boy's matter-of-fact assessment of the aging pet made her smile. "We should all have someone like Sarge watching out for us."

"That's the truth of it, to be sure," Maggie Kinley announced in a voice that carried a faint Irish lilt. Carrying a huge platter filled with thick slices of honey-glazed ham, she came out from behind the gigantic island that separated the long table from the working area of the kitchen. "But for now, anyone who walks around on four paws needs to scoot. Lunch is ready."

Taking their cue from her, Abby and Parker herded the dogs and a cat that had appeared out of nowhere onto a screened-in porch and shut the door to keep them away from the food. The animated discussion of a new horse that had arrived yesterday continued at the table, and some of the details Drew had to share about the animal's poor condition were sobering, to say the least. Heather was grateful to see that Josh had seated Bailey near the other end and slid into the empty spot on the bench beside her, effectively shielding her from the overwhelming sea of strangers. As Heather took the other side, she caught his eye and mouthed, "Thank you."

He responded with one of his bright country boy grins, and she easily returned the gesture. Reserved by nature, she couldn't help noticing that just being around him made her feel more relaxed than she'd been in a very long time.

Leaning in, he nudged Bailey's shoulder. "Kinda crazy around here, huh?"

"Is this your whole family?"

"Nah. We've got aunts, uncles and cousins all over the area, and my mom's parents live a couple of hours away. When everyone gets together, we need a park to hold us all."

"A big park," Heather added.

"There are never so many that we can't make room for more," Maggie assured her, putting the serving platter in the center of the table before taking her seat at the foot. Picking up a bowl of potato salad, she asked, "So, what's new with everyone this week?"

In her peripheral vision, Heather noticed Mike give Lily a look, and she nodded slightly. As he took her hand, his weathered features broke into a grin. "We've got the go-ahead from the doctor to tell everyone now. There's another little Kinley on the way."

Maggie stopped with the serving spoon in midair, staring at him as if he'd just told her he'd found gold in the creek that ran through their property. She let out a delighted squeal and bolted from her chair, rushing to the other end of the table to wrap one arm around Lily and the other around Mike. "It will be so wonderful having a baby in the house again! When are you due?"

"A few weeks after Bekah," Lily answered, sending her sister-in-law a bright smile. "I may need some advice from you as things go along."

"I'd be happy to help out any way I can," Bekah replied, beaming with unabashed joy. "It'll be so fantastic having our kids grow up together."

"As long as they're both girls, it'll be fine," Erin said in a cynical tone. "We've already got more than enough boys around here as it is."

Josh protested in a long groan, but Drew laughed. "No promises on that one, sis. We're gonna find out in the delivery room."

"So are we," Lily said. "This is my first baby, and I love surprises."

While the conversation shifted from horses to nurseries and baby names, it dawned on Heather that her hosts' gracious demeanor extended to more than the retired racehorses and other animals they rescued. Watching Lily and Erin with their children, she never would have guessed that they weren't Abby and Parker's biological mothers. Apparently, where the Kinleys were concerned, family was more than blood.

It was love.

A strong current of it flowed around the people seated at that scarred oak table, encircling even Heather in a warmth that extended far beyond the physical. Now she understood where Josh had come by the generous streak he'd shown her from their very first meeting beside the moving van. This was a family who saw a need and did what they could to meet it. Being connected to these remarkable people, even as an employee of the rescue center, was more than an honor for her.

It was a blessing.

She'd never been one to view things from that perspective, but so many people she'd encountered this week had spoken openly of their faith. After the storm, many of them had expressed the same deep gratitude for Bailey's safety that she'd been experiencing herself. It was gratifying to know that she wasn't the only one who felt that way. After driving herself so hard for so long, it felt good to pause long enough to enjoy the simple things that she and Bailey had clearly been missing out on.

After lunch, the kids recruited Bailey to help with the dishes, and she happily went along as they made it into a game. Being the oldest of the three, Parker finished first and tossed his towel on the counter like a gauntlet. "First one to the pond gets the big inner tube!"

He dashed upstairs, Abby close on his heels. Then, to Heather's amazement, the girl came back to take Bailey's hand. "Come on. I've got an old bathing suit that doesn't fit me anymore. You can borrow it and go swimming, too."

Bailey cast a hesitant look at Heather, and she felt her own heart fall in disappointment. "Thanks for thinking of that, Abby, but we'll have to pass this time. Bailey hasn't learned how to swim yet."

"No problem there," Josh assured her as he

stood up from the table. "I'll be there, and I'm a certified lifeguard."

"Joshua," Maggie scolded in a horrified tone, glaring up at her much-taller son. "Don't tell me you were wearing your swim trunks under your church clothes."

He flashed her a shameless grin, and she shook her head at him. But judging by the fondness sparkling in her hazel eyes, she had a very soft spot for her youngest child.

"I'm not sure what to think of this," Heather teased, which was very unlike her. The heavy responsibilities she carried made her see things much more seriously than most people did. Something about this easygoing farmer made the little girl in her want to come out and play. "Are you really a lifeguard?"

"Scout's honor. And yes," he added before she could test him, "I was a Boy Scout."

"Why do I have no problem believing that?"

Mischief twinkled in those warm blue eyes. "Maybe 'cause I'm so dependable and all. Whataya say?"

"Please, Aunt Heather?" Bailey pleaded, as much with her eyes as her voice. "It would be so much fun, and I promise to be careful."

"All right, but I'll be out there, too. Just in case."

Letting out a delighted whoop, she trailed

after Abby, pounding up the wooden steps as if she'd grown up in the rambling farmhouse instead of arriving only a couple of hours ago.

"That was really nice of Abby to invite her," Heather commented to the girl's parents. "You're raising a thoughtful young lady."

"So are you," Lily responded while she finished wiping down the butcher block island top. "It can't be easy under the circumstances, but you're doing a great job."

"Thank you."

They traded smiles, and for the first time since she'd become Bailey's guardian, Heather felt like an actual parent. It was a terrifying sensation, but also immensely satisfying, and she liked knowing that she was becoming friends with other women who shared her dedication to family.

Heather knew better than most people that when you reached the end of your life, all you had left were the people you loved and who loved you in return. She could have refused her brother's request to be named as Bailey's legal guardian, but it had never even occurred to her. She deeply regretted the tragedy that had turned a workaholic veterinarian into a stand-in mother, but despite the sacrifices of energy and sleep, she had no second thoughts about the path she'd chosen.

If Craig's death had taught her anything, it was that there was nothing in the world more important than family.

Chapter Six

"Look at me, Aunt Heather!" Bailey called out from the center of the small pond. "I'm swimming!"

"I see that, bean," Heather replied, adjusting the video camera on her phone to follow Josh and her through the water. "I'm taking a video so you can see for yourself how well your first lesson is going."

Josh thought their enthusiasm for the very basic skill was cute, and he chuckled when they paused for a rest. "Before too much longer, you'll be having races with Abby and Parker."

"My daddy was going to teach me," Bailey confided quietly. "But he can't now 'cause he's up in heaven with Mommy."

Tears glistened in her eyes, and Josh felt the same reaction he did whenever he saw a pretty girl cry: panic. Anxious to comfort her, he searched for a way to distract her from the sadness he understood all too well. Losing his own father had been tough for him, and he could only imagine how difficult it was for a child to handle that kind of grief.

Recalling his mother's comforting words on the subject, he said, "Y'know, they can see us from up there. And I know your daddy's looking down on you right now, proud as anything."

"Do you really think so?"

"Yeah, I do, but don't take my word for it. My mom told me that when my father died, and she knows just about everything."

He hadn't meant to share quite that much, and he chided himself for upsetting her. He really had to learn to think first and speak later. Another of Mom's lessons he hadn't quite mastered yet.

Bailey pinned him with a thoughtful stare. "Is that why you're so nice to me? Because you know how sad I am?"

"I'm nice to you 'cause you're a cutie pie." Giving her a smile, he ticked the end of her nose with his finger.

"My aunt's a cutie pie," Bailey continued, deftly changing the subject like a pro. "She's really smart, too. Do you like her?"

All on their own, his eyes drifted over to where Heather was sitting on the nearby dock, dangling her bare feet in the water. Wearing a flowery sundress, she looked as if she was ready to grab a basket of sandwiches and head out for a picnic somewhere. The sundress was nothing like the classy, professional clothes he'd seen her in until now, but it suited her perfectly. When she gave him a questioning look, he couldn't help grinning back. "Yeah, she's okay."

"Please," Heather simpered, fanning her face with her hand. "If you don't stop, I may faint."

Having seen her tolerance for gruesome things that would stop most folks in their tracks, Josh couldn't envision her fainting over much of anything. Just another quality that made the cautious city girl unlike any other woman he'd known. Hoping to keep the conversation from getting too personal, he picked up one of Bailey's hands. "I think you're just pruney enough, sweetness. Time for a towel."

He scooped her up and waded over to the dock, lifting her up to where Heather was holding a striped beach towel open wide. Wrapping her niece inside, she gave her the kind of quick hug he'd noticed so many times when they were together. It was obvious that although their new vet wasn't a biological mother, she had a strong instinct for it that extended from her niece to all the animals she'd been treating at the center.

And to him, he realized suddenly. Heather had been a lot more concerned than he had about his injured hand and the bumps and bruises he'd gotten while rescuing Bailey. Over his protests, she'd made sure he was tended to properly. Even more surprising, he'd let her do it. He had to admit he kind of liked her fussing over him. It made him feel…

From out of nowhere, Charlie came bounding toward him in his usual crazy way. Unprepared, Josh lost his balance and flew back into the water with seventy pounds of golden retriever on top of him. As his head went under, he heard Mike bellowing at the dog while Drew laughed from the bank like a maniac. Coming up sputtering, Josh wiped his eyes clear in time to notice Heather hiding a smile in Bailey's towel.

"I saw that, Doc," he said as he swam back in. "Maybe you'd like to see for yourself how funny a dunking is."

"No, thank you."

He hauled himself back onto the dock and took the towel she offered him. It came along with a smile as warm as sunshine, and it struck him that when this very serious woman allowed herself to loosen up, she was by far the prettiest thing he'd ever seen.

Bad, he warned himself firmly. *Very bad*. Admiring her wasn't a problem, but letting himself slide toward anything more than that would be foolish, at best. Aside from Erin's warning, Heather was miles out of his league. While he'd never been opposed to having a little fun, his instincts told him that Heather wasn't the kind of woman you messed around with.

She was the kind you married and built a life with. And since he had no intention of doing that, the smartest approach was to keep their connection nice and light. That way, neither of them would get hurt. He wasn't exactly thrilled with his solution, but since the only other option was to avoid her entirely, he'd have to make it work somehow.

Leaning back on his elbows, he dropped his head back to drink in the warm, breezy day. It was a rare afternoon off for him, and he planned to make the most of it. The sound of bare feet in the grass alerted him that rug rats were about to invade, and he opened one eye to make sure he was prepared for whatever was coming.

Fortunately, it was Abby, who didn't pounce

on him the way Parker would have. "Bailey, Grammy's getting us some Popsicles. Do you want one?"

"Yeah!" As an afterthought, she checked with Heather, who nodded.

As the two girls skipped toward the house, Heather sighed. "I haven't seen her this happy in a long time. I can't thank you and your family enough for making us feel so welcome."

"I'm glad she likes it here. Having a place where you can relax makes things better for both of you."

"Speaking of making things better," she went on in a conversational tone, "the girls and I were chatting earlier, and Lily came up with a great idea to raise the money we need for repairing the playground."

"Doesn't surprise me. If it wasn't for her, Mike never would've even thought about starting the Gallimore Riding School that brings in so much business for the farm. What'd she come up with this time?"

"A committee that can work well together and brainstorm ideas for raising money quickly. She and the others rattled off a list of people they thought might help us out, and Cam offered to let us use the snack bar at the Oaks Café for our meetings."

"And you're telling me this why?"

"You're already doing the construction, and the new market you're pursuing for the farm is inventive and practical. I'm sure if you put your mind to it, you've got more where that came from."

Josh considered the idea and decided it couldn't do any harm—and would in fact do plenty of good for the families in town. "Well, since you put it like that, how could I say no?"

"Thank you!" With a delighted squeal, she hugged him and jumped to her feet. "I'll go tell the girls. They were split fifty-fifty on whether or not I could convince you to agree."

As he watched her run over to join the others around the picnic table, he couldn't keep back a smile. In the end, it wasn't her logic that had swayed him to say yes, or even the niceties she'd been laying on thick enough to hold up a brick wall.

It was how she'd talked about the effort, referring to "we" instead of "they," the way she had when they were first discussing the fund-raising with Erin. Bailey wasn't the only one still reeling from the loss of her father, he knew, although as an adult, Heather was more skilled at hiding her grief behind a cheerful demeanor and a busy schedule.

Still struggling to adapt to her new life, she seemed to be searching for a place where she and Bailey could find some calm and catch their breath. Being involved in a grassroots event was a small thing, but it was a start. And if she believed that he could do something to help that along, he was happy to oblige.

Footsteps came up behind him, and he wasn't surprised when his brothers dropped down to sit on each side of him.

"Fund-raising committee?" Drew scoffed. "Since when do you do stuff like that?"

Josh shrugged. "The lady asked me to help raise some money for the playground, so I'm going along."

"And getting more time with her in the bargain," Drew filled in the painfully obvious blank. "I thought Erin warned you to stay away from Heather so we don't have to worry about any complications at the rescue center."

"This is different. It's for Bailey and the other kids. Like your daughter," he said, aiming his retort in Mike's direction.

That got him a long, uncomfortable look from his savvy big brother. "So you'd be doing this even if Lily was asking you instead of Heather?"

"Sure. I don't get why it's such a big deal to have me there, but if the girls think that me being involved will make a difference, I'm game. Besides," he added with a grin, "no one in their right mind says no to your wife. Getting people to cooperate is her superpower."

"He's got a point there," Drew admitted, chuckling again. "She's got a way of making it sound like you're doing her a personal favor."

"Yeah, she does," Mike agreed with a grin of his own. "That's how we ended up together in the first place."

"On that note, my wife looks like she's ready to drop. I'm gonna take her home and get her off her feet. Catch ya later."

Drew sauntered over to the picnic table, leaving Josh and Mike alone.

"So did I pass?" Josh asked wryly. "Is the interrogation over?"

"For now, but you need to keep something in mind." When Mike's voice took on that I'm-in-charge tone, anyone with a lick of sense listened closely. "The Fitzgeralds have been through a lot already this year, and chances are there are more tough days to come. The last thing they need is to have someone stroll in and out of their lives and leave a mess behind. Got it?"

Josh prickled at the suggestion that he might do something so heartless. "What're you getting at?"

"That woman over there—" he nodded toward where Heather was sitting "—is gonna need a lot of patience and understanding. You're a good guy, Josh, but I don't think you're ready to take on that kind of relationship. She's a lot more complicated than the girls you've dated before, and I don't want to see either of you—or Bailey—get hurt."

At a loss for a response, Josh fell back on an old standard. "That won't happen. We're just friends."

Letting out a heavy sigh, Mike stood and stared down at Josh. "If you honestly believe that, you're in even more trouble than I thought."

With that, Mike left him there wondering what on earth was wrong with his family. Erin, and now both of his brothers, seemed to be misjudging the depth of his connection to Heather. Sure, she was gorgeous, not to mention smart and impossible to fool. And she was new in town, which made her more interesting to him than the women he'd grown up with. And Bailey was a definite plus, adorable and funny in a way that made him wonder if Heather had been like her when she was a girl.

But no matter how it might look to anyone else, he and the softhearted vet were exactly what he'd claimed: friends. Still, in the back of his mind, a soft voice he'd never heard before whispered something that made him wonder.

What if?

What if they tried being more and it was awesome? Or just as likely, what if they tried being more and it was a disaster?

Shedding the towel, he stood and whistled for Charlie. Once the dog had galloped over, Josh grabbed his rolled leather collar and pointed toward the middle of the pond.

"Ready?" Letting out a panting whine, the dog danced in place and yelped his answer. Josh laughed, then straightened and let him loose. "Go!"

The two of them barreled down the dock side by side and dived into the water. When he surfaced, Josh was impressed to find that the retriever had bobbed up about two feet in front of him. He swam over and rewarded the dog with a hug. "Nice job, dude. I give it a ten."

He heard feminine laughter and looked over to find Heather watching them from the bank. "Now if you can teach him synchronized swimming, you'll really have something."

"You never know," Josh replied as he swam over to the side. "He's pretty smart when he wants to be."

"And when he doesn't?"

"He puts on a good clueless face, but it's mostly an act."

"Really?" Tilting her head, she gave him a curious look. "Why does he do that?"

From her tone, Josh realized that she assumed he wasn't talking only about the dog. Now that he thought about it, maybe she was right. Normally, he was straightforward with people, but ever since she'd shown up, he'd found himself second-guessing all kinds of things that usually came naturally to him. "Well, he's always been kind of a clown, and folks are used to him being that way."

"Isn't maturing a good thing?"

"Sometimes. But he's got a good heart, and he doesn't want to disappoint anyone."

"Hmm," she commented in a pensive voice. "I wonder what makes him think they wouldn't like him being smart?"

Thankfully, his canine buddy paddled over to rescue Josh from a conversation that had quickly risen over his head. "Maybe you should ask him."

"Maybe I will," she said, adding the kind of feminine smirk that he couldn't begin to interpret. Half knowing, half something else entirely, it made him more nervous than he'd been around a girl since middle school.

Bailey called her name from where she was spinning on the tire swing, and as Heather walked over to admire her technique, Josh let out a long, frustrated breath.

It was possible that Mike and Drew were right about his feelings for Heather, after all. He really hated when that happened.

Wednesday evening, Josh stopped at Pampered Paws on his way to the playground committee meeting at the Oaks Café. He found his mother behind the counter with Parker, who was showing her something on the computer.

"See, Grammy," he explained patiently while she peered over her reading glasses at the monitor, "when you find a new recipe you want to try, you hit this link and send it to the email I set up for you. Then you can print it out and make it for us."

"Just like that?" When he nodded, she gave him the quick embrace that Josh recalled from his own childhood. "Such a clever young man you are. Thank you for showing me."

"This one for marble cookies isn't hard," he said in a nudging tone. "You could take Bailey and me to the store to get the ingredients, and we'll help you make it while you're watching us tonight."

"What a wonderful idea," she said as Heather and Bailey came down the stairs from their apartment. "Would you like to help Parker and me try out a new recipe, Bailey?"

The little girl stood on tiptoe to see what all the fuss was about, and her eyes rounded with interest. "Those look really good."

"Grammy's will be even better," Parker assured her confidently. "Just wait and see."

"Then we'd best get started," Maggie said briskly, holding out a hand for each of them. "Let's see if we can finish them before the grown-ups are done with their meeting."

"Save me some, would ya?" Josh asked, rubbing his stomach.

Parker gave him a sour look, and Maggie laughed. "We'll make an extra batch, so there will be plenty for all of us. We'll see you up in Heather's apartment when you're finished."

As she left with her assistant chefs, Erin stood at the counter, shaking her head. "I guess the way to a guy's heart really is through his stomach."

"Mine, anyway," Josh teased, strolling over to open the door. "Cam's gonna feed us, right?"

"Didn't you have dinner?" his sister demanded.

"I only had five minutes, so it was shower or eat. I figured people would like it better if I was clean."

She wrinkled her nose and sailed past him,

muttering something unflattering as she went. Grinning, Josh turned his attention to Heather. "And how was your day?"

"Busy, but I'm starting to get the hang of how the center operates."

He picked up on the hesitation in her voice. "You sound a little nervous, Doc."

"I am. I don't know anyone outside of your family, so this could be awful."

"Or it could be awesome. You never know."

She gave him the skeptical look that he'd quickly learned was more habit than part of her character. "Are you always so positive?"

"Mostly. Some folks think it's annoying."

"Well, I think it's sweet. I hope you never lose it."

Beneath the cautionary tone he caught a thread of warmth, and he couldn't keep back a smile. "I'll do my best."

The café stood next to Erin's shop, and as they walked through the open double doors, they discovered that the committee of a dozen had taken over a corner booth in the main dining room. Cam stood at one end, arms folded while he listened to his wife do what she did best. Take charge.

"So, any ideas, we want to hear them," she was saying when Josh and Heather came in to stand beside Cam. Erin's eyes flicked over, and she stood up to put a big sisterly arm around the new girl in town. "Everyone, I'd like you to meet our fabulous new veterinarian, Heather Fitzgerald. We keep her pretty busy at the rescue center, but she and her niece, Bailey, have generously offered to help with our fund-raising effort. Why don't we go around the table and introduce ourselves?"

She nodded first to the Sheppards, whom Heather had already met. Josh silently thanked his sister for starting off easy to give Heather some confidence before getting to the strangers. Once they were all acquainted, Heather sat next to Erin, and he slid in next to her supportively, which earned him a grateful smile from their guest.

"Now, on to why we're all here," Erin continued. "How to generate a bunch of money in a hurry."

The list began with the usual, including a community yard sale that Josh privately suspected was a way for people to simultaneously get rid of stuff they didn't want and donate the money to a good cause. None of the suggestions got a lot of support, and he was beginning to wonder if the townsfolk had finally run out of new ideas.

Then, to his surprise, Heather raised her hand halfway, like a kid who wasn't sure she knew the answer but was willing to take a shot. When Erin nodded at her, Heather took a quiet breath and said, "I've been thinking about this, and I came up with something that might be fun. A bachelor dance auction."

The group rustled with interest, and Erin prompted her to explain.

"When I was in college, my sorority's house needed a new roof and we didn't have the money for it. We collaborated with a fraternity to allow their members to be auctioned off for a dance with the highest bidder. It was very popular, and we made a lot of money. They got a percentage of our profits, and we got a new roof."

"We've got plenty of bachelors in town," Louise Sheppard commented, rattling off several names. Others added more, and Erin scribbled furiously, trying to capture them all.

Josh was enjoying the whole thing until he realized that Heather was eyeballing him. From the calculating look on her face, he figured she had a particular bachelor in mind. Fortunately for him, Erin chose that moment to call for a break, and he stood to escort Heather away from the table for a private word.

"Seriously? Me?"

"You're a bachelor, aren't you? Besides, I've noticed how the girls in town start drooling whenever they see you. You'd probably bring in a small fortune all by yourself."

"Well, now, that's real flattering," he admitted, grinning at the compliment. "What would I have to do?"

"To make it more of an event, we should let women register for a chance to bid on a dance with their favorite bachelor. It will generate interest and encourage people to attend to see who wins. We can have refreshments and a raffle to bump up the total, but the real draw will be you. All of you," she clarified quickly.

"One problem, darlin'." She tilted her head in anticipation. "I don't dance."

"Oh, come on," she scoffed with a laugh. "You must've managed to do a little of it at your prom, or at a family wedding or something."

"Nope. I know my strengths, and that ain't one of 'em."

She took a few moments to absorb his revelation, then gave him one of those feminine looks any guy worth his salt knew meant trouble. "What if I taught you? Then would you agree to be part of the auction?"

"Are you nuts? My feet are twice the size of yours. I'd probably crush every one of your toes in the first ten minutes."

"It's not that hard to learn a basic waltz. You

count to three and make your steps match the music. It's not like you have to be able to do the tango or anything complicated like that." Her smile deepening, she went in for the kill. "Let's be honest. Any girl who's bidding on a dance with you is going to be much more interested in flirting with you than in how well you dance."

"So you're gonna dangle me out there like a big ol' piece of meat at the zoo, is that it?"

"For charity," she reminded him with a sly smile. "To rebuild the playground for the kids in time for summer vacation. It wouldn't surprise me in the least if the money you bring in puts us over the top."

"Well, since you put it like that, how could I say no?"

What a difference a few days can make, Heather thought as she pulled into the clinic's parking lot the following Friday morning. She and Bailey had been in their new home almost two weeks now, and they'd gradually settled into a routine that seemed to work for them. Thanks to the kind residents of Oaks Crossing—especially the Kinleys—Bailey was finally beginning to show signs of overcoming the tragedy that had yanked her father out of her life so abruptly.

Because she was less worried about her niece, Heather was coming to terms with her own grief, and it felt like things were on the upswing for both of them. One of the best moments came when she walked through the clinic's front door with a very welcome guest.

"No way!" Sierra cheered, hurrying around the tall counter to greet her. "Is this the same kitten?"

After some long nights and plenty of TLC, it was hard to recognize the bedraggled foundling in the fluffy, playful creature Annabelle had become. Blinking against the fluorescent lights, she gazed up at the vet tech with wide eyes that had changed into a brilliant blue that Heather knew would be their permanent color. Offering up a dainty meow, she cocked her head in a pose so adorable, Heather was fairly certain that the little darling could win a prize just about anywhere.

"Oh, look at you," Bekah crooned, reaching out to take her. Pulling her in close, the mom-to-be sighed as the kitten playfully pawed her cheek. "What a sweetheart you are."

"I thought she might like to come and get acquainted with her littermates," Heather explained in a professional manner that clearly wasn't fooling either of them. Giving in, she laughed. "Okay, I thought it would be fun if we could all have a turn playing with her. Happy?"

"I knew there was a good heart in there the second I met you," Sierra announced.

"You sound surprised by that."

"Well," the young woman hedged, then seemed to decide it was time to fess up. "Your résumé was really impressive, and during your online interview with Erin that I sat in on, you seemed kind of—"

After a moment, Heather prodded, "Kind of what? It's okay to be honest with me, Sierra. I can take it."

"Chilly," Bekah answered for her, quickly adding, "but then we met you and it was obvious that we just had a bad connection that day. Satellite images can be tricky sometimes, and we don't get the best reception here in the hills."

"Unfortunately, that's not the first time I've heard that from someone," Heather confided with a frown. "My mom always says it's my light hair and eyes that make me look icy when people first meet me."

"Sure," Sierra agreed immediately, nodding. "That's it."

"But after talking to you for five seconds, folks know otherwise," Bekah chimed in with a smile.

She appreciated their attempts to make her feel better, and she tried to brush off their errant first opinion of her by picking up the clipboard that held their updated schedule for the day. In truth, their revelation pricked her ego more than she'd like to admit. But since there was nothing she could do about people's views of her, she decided it was best to move on.

"Anyway," she began in an upbeat tone as she glanced over the handwritten sheet, "is there anything going on today that I need to know about?"

As if in response, the roar of a tractor interrupted their morning briefing. The sudden racket scared Annabelle, and she cowered against Bekah, trying to dig into the sleeve of her T-shirt in search of a safe place to hide.

"Oh, that's right," Sierra commented with a laugh. "Josh is bringing some hay in for the baby barn this morning."

Heather had gotten a full tour of the various sections of the rescue center, but she hadn't had the time to fully explore the area the staff had given such an appealing nickname. Glancing around, she said, "It looks like you have things under control out here. If you don't mind, I'd like to get a better look at how you do things for the wild ones."

"No problem," Sierra replied. "While you're

there, check out the otter family that came in last night. A mama with three babies—they're adorable."

"Otters don't spend much of their time on dry land. How do you manage to keep them in a barn?"

"Oh, we're pretty resourceful around here. Go find out for yourself."

Intrigued by the cryptic answer, Heather tucked a dozing Annabelle against her shoulder and walked down the hallway that led to the adjacent barn. There, she found young critters ranging from an orphaned skunk to a pair of fox kits that one of the day care teachers had found curled up in a corner of her garden shed.

Heather took her time wandering through, admiring the clever enclosures that kept each species safely corralled away from the rest but gave them enough space to roam around. Inside a walled-off spot that had once been a horse's stall, she found their newest arrivals and couldn't resist going inside for a closer look.

There, lounging on her back in a bright yellow kiddie pool, a sleek brown otter was floating with three dozing pups sprawled across her stomach. Mama's front left paw was wrapped in a splint and bandage, and there were telltale stains from the antiseptic that had been used to clean a neatly stitched gash on her jaw. Her wary eyes glittered like obsidian, and it didn't take much imagination to understand that she was assessing whether or not Heather posed a threat to her brood.

"You're all right, Mama," she murmured gently. "No one here is going to hurt you or your babies."

The otter's whiskers caught the light while her nose twitched, as if she was considering what Heather had told her. Then, apparently satisfied, she closed her eyes and resumed her napping.

A low chuckle rumbled behind her. "Cute, huh?"

"Very." Turning, Heather met Josh's warm blue eyes on the other side of the wooden partition. "I'm wondering how they ended up here, though."

"When the weather's so nice, folks are outdoors a lot. A guy found this crew next to his favorite fishing hole, and the mother looked like she'd gone a round or two with something nasty. So he scooped up the whole clan and brought 'em here. Our wildlife rehabber figures they'll be ready to go back to where they came from in a couple of weeks."

"That's wonderful," Heather said, smiling as Annabelle stretched out with a yawning meow before curling into a sleepy ball again. "Everyone here does such good work."

Grinning, Josh ran a finger over the kitten's forehead. "So do you. From the way she looks now, you'd never guess she was so bad off when she first came in."

"I guess we make a good team." As soon as she said it, Heather realized those words could easily be misinterpreted and hastened to add, "I mean, the staff and me. I didn't expect to feel this comfortable in a new place so quickly. It's nice."

"It sure is."

Something else twinkled in his eyes, and she wondered if there was more that he wanted to say to her. She waited for him to continue, but when he didn't, she jumped in to fill the awkward silence. "So, I hear you're bringing in some hay for us?"

"Yeah. I was checking on my new cornfield, then started baling and remembered that the feed barn was getting low last time I was here. I dropped most of it off there and brought the rest down so I don't have to make an emergency run later on."

"How's your special corn doing?"

"Better than I expected. Prices are holding steady for now, so the end result looks promising. I told Mike about it yesterday, and he was impressed."

"Good for you." Then what he'd said about his schedule sank in, and she asked, "You were in the fields earlier this morning, when it was dark?" He nodded as if hours of extra work were no big deal to him. "How do you see what you're doing?"

"Well, now," he replied in an exaggerated drawl, "a few years back they came up with these newfangled things called headlights. They do the job, and then some."

Before she knew what she was doing, Heather rolled her eyes and made a face that she hadn't used since she was about ten years old. It was childish and unprofessional, and she immediately regretted it. "Josh, I'm sorry. That was rude."

"No, it was funny," he corrected her with a grin. "I didn't know you had that kind of sass in you, so it was a cool surprise."

Cool surprise? Had he really just complimented her for acting like a brat? Raised to behave properly no matter the circumstances, she wasn't sure what to make of his reaction. Then again, the Kinleys had all struck her as casual, friendly people who tolerated a wide range of personalities, from reserved Mike to assertive Erin to the unapologetic smart aleck Drew.

Clearly, Josh had learned a different way of living than she had, which probably explained his grounded, easygoing attitude. Her strict upbringing and ambitious goals had made her who she was, and she was proud of what she'd accomplished. But now that she'd met someone from a background so markedly different from her own, she couldn't help wondering if in being so driven, she'd been missing out on something just as important.

She'd adored Bailey from the moment she was born, but now their relationship had a deeper significance for both of them. They'd always been family, but now they *were* a family, albeit a small one. Since this was new territory for Heather, she figured it couldn't hurt to learn a thing or two from a large, loving group like the Kinleys.

"Heather?"

When her brain looped back to the present, she realized that Josh had been waiting for her to say something. "Hmm?"

"I meant that as a good thing," he confided with a sheepish look. "You might not've taken it that way, though. If you didn't, I apologize."

His forlorn expression made her think of a big, overzealous dog who was dreading a scolding for jumping up and ruining her dress. "No, you were fine. I've just never heard anyone say that about me, so I wasn't sure how to respond. You like sassy women?"

She hadn't meant to add that last part out loud, and she cringed at how it sounded. Then, to her astonishment, he laughed.

"Are you kidding? Have you met the ladies in my family? Loads of spunk, every last one of 'em. Even Abby."

That was a dodge if ever she'd heard one, and she tilted her head in a chiding gesture. "You didn't exactly answer my question."

Grinning now, he rested his elbows on the wall between them and leaned in close enough for her to catch the scent of straw and sunshine this charming country boy carried with him everywhere he went. "Yeah, I like sassy women. There aren't enough of you in the world, far as I'm concerned."

His gaze held hers with no effort at all, softening as it roamed over her face. The smile lighting his features mellowed into one that was less flirtatious and more something she couldn't quite identify.

"I—well—" Mortified by her stammering, she drew herself up and tried to gather up the shreds of her feminine dignity. "Thank you."

"You're welcome."

Standing to his full height, he flashed her one last knee-weakening grin before turning and sauntering back to where a half-empty hay wagon stood waiting for him to unload and get back to his baling. Feeling like a complete moron, Heather debated whether or not to follow him and explain her sudden, embarrassing bout of brainlessness. After a few seconds, she decided against it and headed out the way she'd come in.

She dropped Annabelle off to visit her siblings in their blanket-lined box and then gladly immersed herself in work. Having endured so many years of rigorous schooling and demanding practicums, she loved being able to put her training into practice every day. The difference was that, here, she was tending to animals that no one wanted in an effort to make them healthy enough to be adopted later.

During her lunch break, she added a note to the to-do list she kept on her phone. *Contact wildlife rehabber re: lessons.* The Oaks Crossing Rescue Center's dual purpose offered her a unique opportunity to familiarize herself with patients beyond the usual pets and other domesticated creatures. She didn't know what type of animal hospital she'd end up in down the road, and being comfortable with treating wild animals just might put her over the top in comparison with the other candidates who applied for the same position.

Beyond that, it would be fun.

Where had that come from? she wondered, shaking her head at the foolish idea. Pragmatic by nature as much as by habit, everything she did had a purpose and a price that she'd thoroughly examined ahead of time. These days, she was up to her neck in student loan debt and had a niece to raise. While she had Craig's life insurance in the bank, that money was earmarked for Bailey, to make sure she'd have as secure a future as Heather could give her.

Sometimes being the grown-up was hard, but someone had to do it, and by default the role was hers. Bailey was counting on her, and she'd do it to the best of her ability, the same way she did everything else.

The rest of the day flew by, and when Heather was finished, she went to collect Annabelle. Over the Dutch door, she saw quite possibly the most adorable scene ever. Bekah had given a couple of female lop-eared rabbits the run of the small space, and one of them had taken up residence on a corner of the kittens' fluffy blanket.

Annabelle had obviously woken up to find that she was sharing space with someone new and was cautiously creeping over to investigate. The rabbit sat totally still, her twitching nose the only evidence that she wasn't a life-like statue in someone's garden. Sniffing the air between them with each tiny step, Annabelle sat next to the rabbit, ears perked as she cocked her head in feline fascination. Because her eyes were on the sides of her head, the bunny had an excellent peripheral view without having to move.

When Annabelle mewed, the rabbit crinkled her forehead in disapproval but didn't seem to be irritated enough to move. Apparently, the cat interpreted that as a gesture of friendship and plopped herself down shoulder-to-shoulder with her new buddy, rubbing her cheek over the soft fur in obvious appreciation.

Heather caught the sound of muted laughter behind her and turned to find Sierra holding up her phone, video camera rolling. The tech lifted a finger to her lips and pointed to the touching scene that she'd been filming. Heather nodded her understanding and waited a couple of minutes until the rabbit got tired of being adored and hopped away to join her cotton-tailed friend on the other side of the room.

Sierra tapped the button to end her video and let out the laughter she'd been holding in. "That's about the cutest thing I've seen the whole time I've been working here. We'll have Bekah fix the lighting and post it in the adoption section of the website. Those rabbits should have a new home by Monday."

"That would be fantastic," Heather said as she checked the area in front of the door before opening it to retrieve the kitten. Touching noses with her, she asked, "What do you say, little miss? Are you ready to go pick up Bailey?"

Annabelle responded with a half meow, half yawn that made the two women laugh.

"Have a good weekend, boss." Waving, Sierra headed into the kennel to start bedding down the residents for the night.

Heather stopped to say goodbye to Bekah and a high schooler who came in to help out three days a week. The center had a small army of volunteers, and while she'd gotten to know some of them, most still blurred together in her memory. That didn't feel right to her, and as she drove into town, she made a mental note to ask her full-timers for a list of everyone who worked at the center and some hints on how to keep them all straight.

Driving past the town park, she noticed that the demolition of the playground had started. The worst of the damaged beams were gone, leaving a thin skeleton of what had been a sturdy compound of towers, bridges and slides. Abby's beloved pirate ship had been reduced to a pile of kindling, and while she'd never been there herself, Heather felt saddened by the sight of what had been destroyed. It would take a lot of sweat and skill to return the playground to its original state, she thought somberly.

That reminded her of the deal she and Bailey had made with Josh in return for him donating his time and labor to the project. She'd have to check in with Erin and see if the bachelor auction dance had been scheduled. If the early enthusiasm she'd been hearing was any indication, the women in town were looking forward to the event, and it would probably end up being their biggest source of cash. Something like that never would've flown in Detroit, she mused as she pulled into the church parking lot. It was just one more example of the 180-degree turn her life had taken since she'd connected with Erin Kinley.

It hadn't taken long for the quaintness of Oaks Crossing to grow on Heather. But like everyone else, she had bills to pay, and even though their apartment was free, she could stretch her modest salary only so far. Once her larger loan payments started up this time next year, her financial situation would go from grim to deadly.

Until then, she'd take the opportunity to

enjoy this small Kentucky town with Bailey. There was no point being gloomy before it was absolutely necessary.

"Hello, Dr. Fitzgerald!" Tammy Sheppard greeted her with more energy than any adult should have after a day spent leading a class of preschoolers. "How are you this afternoon?"

"Fine, thanks. And you?"

"We had a blast today. Mrs. Wheaton—our pastor's wife—came in and gave us a music lesson. I'll let Bailey tell you the details."

"Okay." Heather didn't understand the need for secrecy, but before she could question the teacher, her niece came racing over and into Heather's arms. "Hey there, bean. I hear you had a fun day."

"I learned a song on the piano!" Bailey exclaimed, eyes dancing in excitement. "And Cara Simon invited me to sleep over on Saturday. Can I go? Pleeease?"

"Wow," Heather stalled, trying to get her bearings. She caught movement out of the corner of her eye and turned to find a professionally dressed woman gliding toward them on to-die-for designer heels.

"Hi, Dr. Fitzgerald, I'm Joanna Simon, Cara's mother." Offering a hand that sported some dazzling rings and an antique gold watch, she added an apologetic smile. "I told the girls it would be more appropriate if I called you later to ask you myself, but you know how kids are when they get excited."

"Sure."

"I'm a family court judge over in Rockville," the woman went on. "We moved to town last month, so Cara is new here and hasn't had the easiest time fitting in. She goes on and on about what a great friend Bailey has been to her. We were hoping to show our gratitude by having Bailey over for dinner and some movies. All G-rated, of course."

"Of course."

"We'll be home all day tomorrow and Sunday, so if she wants, she's welcome to spend the night with us. We live on Main Street, too, so we're not far away if she decides she'd rather be in her own bed. We can just play that by ear."

"I want to stay, Aunt Heather," Bailey insisted breathlessly. "I've never had a sleepover, and it would be so much fun."

"I'm glad to hear that, honey, and I know Cara would love it, too," the judge said, giving her a warm smile. "But if you change your mind, just speak up and we'll take you home."

Heather thought five years old was a little young for staying over at a friend's house, but Bailey was so thrilled by the idea, Heather couldn't bear to disappoint her by saying no. "Thanks so much for inviting her, Mrs. Simon. Should she bring anything special?"

"It's Joanna, and just send her regular overnight things," the woman replied airily, waving as if a girl's first night away from home was no big deal. "We're not fancy, so whatever's comfortable for Bailey is fine with us."

Heather eyed her niece, who was bouncing in place like a helium balloon ready to break free of its tether. What harm could there be? Best case, she'd have a fabulous time with her new friend. Worst case, Heather would travel a few blocks to retrieve her in the middle of the night.

Feeling a bit more confident now, she smiled. "What time would you like me to drop her off?"

"We have some errands and appointments in the afternoon, so you can come by around six." Grasping her daughter's hand, Joanna waved. "We'll see you then."

Before Heather knew it, she and Bailey had collected everything from her cubby and were opening the door to their apartment. Her whirling dervish of a niece blew through the living room and dumped the contents of her backpack onto her bed, all while listing what she needed to take with her to Cara's.

Amused by the whole thing, Heather poured formula into a saucer for Annabelle and hung back until Bailey announced, "Okay, I'm ready."

"That's great, bean, but you know you're not going until tomorrow, right?"

"I just want to be ready."

Heather wished she had that much energy at the end of a day. She grinned. "Okay, but let's check and make sure you've got everything." Rummaging through the hastily packed bag, she couldn't help laughing. "You've got some fun games and your favorite stuffed animals. What about your pj's and clean clothes for Sunday?"

Bailey blinked at her, and a sheepish grin crept along her freckled cheeks. "I forgot."

While they gathered up the extra things, Annabelle sashayed into the room to see what was going on. Obviously confused by all the commotion, she sat down on her haunches, pawing to get up on the bed. Bailey gently picked her up and set her on the pillow before turning to Heather. "She likes to sleep under the covers. Will you let her do that in your room, just for tomorrow night?"

It finally seemed to have occurred to her that she'd be away from home for the first time, and her excitement had dimmed a bit. Heather's own emotions were starting to do the same, and she forced a bright smile for her niece's sake. "Of course I will. I'll even let her pick out a movie to watch."

"She likes *The Aristocats*," Bailey informed her in a very grown-up voice. "And if you don't keep an eye on her, she'll chew the books you keep on your night table."

"Gotcha."

Saturday raced by in a flurry of laundry, art projects and hunting high and low for Annabelle when she somehow got lost in the small apartment. After finding her asleep in a corner of Bailey's closet, Heather realized that it was nearly time to take Bailey to the Simons'. Where had the day gotten to? Sometimes she really missed those college years when she'd spent her Saturdays hanging out in the student lounge or shopping with friends.

Ignoring the rare bout of self-pity, she called out, "Bailey, it's almost six! Are you ready to go?"

She got an eager shout in reply, and Bailey charged into the living room wearing her backpack and carrying her fluffy pink pillow. Since the Simons lived so close, they walked up Main Street toward the address Joanna had given Heather yesterday. A lovely center-hall Colonial rose up behind a wrought iron fence that framed a big yard and a herringbone-patterned brick walkway lined with flowers. It was early May, and up north the weather could still be cool at night, so gardens were a long way from looking their best. Here in Kentucky, everything was already in full bloom. Something else to like about Oaks Crossing, Heather mused with a smile.

"This is such a pretty house." Bailey echoed her thoughts almost perfectly. "Maybe we could have one like this someday."

"That would be fabulous," Heather agreed heartily as she rang the doorbell.

Unfortunately, she added silently, until she paid off her student debts, their home would have to be a modestly priced apartment. Or free, as it was now. Yet another plus for this quaint little town. She couldn't help noticing that they kept adding up, making her current situation even more appealing to her.

Her meandering thoughts were interrupted by the thudding of feet inside, just before the inside door swung open to reveal a breathless dark-haired girl about Bailey's age. A female voice sounded in the background, and Cara took a deep breath before saying, "Hello, Dr. Fitzgerald. Welcome to our home."

Heather often received compliments from other adults about how polite Bailey was, but

Cara's greeting was almost black-tie formal. Not wanting to hurt the girl's feelings by showing her amusement, Heather smothered a grin. "Thank you, Cara. And thank you for inviting Bailey over. She's very excited."

"Please, come in." Opening the door wide, she stepped back to let them through.

When Joanna appeared behind her, the judge was beaming proudly. "Very nice, honey. Why don't you take Bailey up to your room so she can put her things away?"

"Okay."

More childlike now, Cara grabbed Bailey's pillow and bolted up the elegant stairway with Bailey close on her heels.

"I love that child," Joanna said with an indulgent smile. "She's a handful sometimes, but she's the light at the end of every day for me. Sometimes, knowing I'll see her is all that gets me through."

"It must be tough, with the kind of work you do," Heather sympathized. "As Bailey's guardian, I have some experience in the family law system. It's pretty complex, and I can only imagine how difficult it must be to deal with it on a daily basis."

"You're right about that, but it can also be very rewarding. My husband is a family therapist, so we're committed to helping children and their parents in any way we can."

"That can't be easy. I really admire both of you."

The lovely woman beamed in gratitude. "Thank you. After the week I had, you have no idea how much that means to me. But I'm sure you have things to do with your free evening. Why don't we exchange contact information so you can be on your way?"

It took them only a few seconds to beam the data to one another, and then Heather said goodbye. Only after she'd left the Simons' immaculate yard and was strolling up the sidewalk did it hit her.

She had nothing to do.

Nowhere she needed to be, no dinner to make, no new art project to gush over. When she caught the scent of something delicious wafting from the Oaks Café, she paused outside the open double doors and considered whether or not to treat herself to dinner.

Why not? she finally decided, pivoting to head inside. She'd been living next to Cam's diner all this time and hadn't eaten there except for snacks at committee meetings. Tonight seemed as good a time as any to sample the full menu. Early as it was, the place was about half-full, with several tables still vacant.

Someone called her name, and she spun around to find Josh Kinley waving at her from a table by the bay window.

Ever the gentleman, he stood and waited for her while she threaded her way over to him. Motioning to the empty chair, he asked, "You look a little lost. Would you like to join me?"

Lost? She rolled the word around in her head, then acknowledged that was exactly what she'd been feeling. These days, her life revolved around the clinic and Bailey, and now that she had some alone time, she didn't quite know what to do with herself. "Thanks. That would be great."

"So," Josh began as he handed her a menu from the rack. "Where's your cute sidekick?"

"At her friend Cara Simon's for a sleepover. I wasn't sure about it, though. I'm worried she's a bit young to be doing that." The confession dredged up her earlier concerns, and she discreetly checked her phone for a possible SOS from Joanna. The screen was blank, and although she knew she should be relieved, she couldn't help feeling a little disappointed.

"They're good folks, and they handle children and teenagers all day long, so Bailey will be fine with them. She's a great kid, and she's making friends. Isn't that why you brought her here in the first place?"

"Of course."

Cocking his head, he grinned. "But?"

He seemed to understand that she was wrestling with emotions she hadn't encountered before. She had no idea how he knew that, but the sympathy in his eyes made her feel more open to confiding in him. "I want her to be strong and independent, so she'll have the confidence she needs later on in life. I just wasn't ready for her to start wanting that kind of freedom now."

"Kids have a knack for surprising grownups. It's part of their charm."

"Meaning that it's going to keep happening?"

"Yup," he said as their waitress arrived. "Better get used to it."

The straightforward advice made perfect sense to her, but that didn't mean she had to like it. Once they'd placed their orders, he poured them each a glass of sweet tea from the pitcher the waitress had left for them.

Heather's first sip of the Southern concoction made her hum in appreciation. "Ooh, that's good. I'm not a big fan of iced tea, but this is delicious."

"Cam puts something special in it. Secret ingredient he won't tell anyone."

She took another sip, swirling it around before swallowing. "I think it's mint."

"Sure, but what kind? Even Erin doesn't know what he uses, and she's married to the guy."

That led their light conversation to his family, and how things were going at the rescue center and the farm. Before she knew it, they'd chatted their way through dinner and homemade cheesecake topped with fresh blackberries, juice drizzling down the sides into a puddle on the plate.

"Cam's mother is a genius in the kitchen," Josh said. "She's had two strokes, so she works at home and has him pick up the desserts a couple of times a day. She says baking is the best therapy she's ever done. Plus, we all get to enjoy her cooking, so it's a win-win."

"Two strokes?" Heather echoed, shaking her head. "How did she and her family ever get through all that?"

"Faith."

The answer came so quickly, she knew it was reflexive for him. Gazing across the table at this handsome, good-hearted man, she said, "You make it sound like religion makes hard things easy."

"Not easy," he corrected her gently, "possible. We all need extra strength at one time or another, like you did when your brother died. Bailey was counting on you, and you stepped up. It wasn't what you had planned, but you did it anyway. The way I see it, God was watching over the two of you, even if you didn't realize it."

Was that really how she'd gotten through that heart-wrenching time? Devastated by the loss of her only sibling, somehow Heather had kept trudging forward. Making funeral and legal arrangements, consoling her parents, doing everything in her power to make Bailey feel safe and loved. Doing what needed to be done because it was important and she was the only one capable of doing it. More than one person had asked her how she'd managed, and because she honestly hadn't known, she'd learned to smile and change the subject.

Was it possible that God had been giving her the strength she needed to survive the worst time in her life? "I hadn't considered that. Does God really work that way?"

"He works in all kinds of ways," Josh assured her, leaning back in his chair so the waitress could clear the table. "If you're interested, you and Bailey are welcome to join us at church on Sunday. Maybe you'll find your answer there."

"I don't know." She hedged. "I haven't been to a service in years."

"Mrs. Wheaton teaches the Sunday school.

They mostly paint pictures and sing kids' worship songs. Bailey would probably love it."

The name rang a bell, and Heather smiled. "Is that the same Mrs. Wheaton who gave the day care classes a singing lesson today?"

"Probably. She never misses a chance to teach kids about music."

"She sounds like my sister-in-law," Heather commented sadly. "Polly was a concert pianist when she met Craig, but when they got serious about each other, she didn't want to put all of her time into performing. She switched her major and became a teacher. No matter how fussy Bailey was, if Polly started singing to her, she'd calm right down, as if she wanted to hear every note."

Heather felt her chin starting to tremble, and she fought to contain a rush of tears that was threatening to break free of her control. Embarrassed, she looked down at the checked tablecloth to avoid Josh's gaze. To her astonishment, a large hand settled over hers for a comforting squeeze.

"It's okay, Heather," he said gently. "Missing people is part of loving them. But as long as you and Bailey keep her parents' memories alive, they won't ever really be gone."

Glancing over, she saw true empathy dimming his usually bright blue eyes. Swallowing hard, she dredged up a wan smile. "Considering what your family's been through, I guess you know what you're talking about."

"Loving people is hard. Losing them is harder. Hanging on to what we get in between is important, 'cause none of us knows how much time we're gonna have together."

"I thought you were a farmer, but just then you sounded like a philosopher."

"Maybe I'm a little of both," he said with a wink.

The lighthearted gesture blew away some of her sadness, and she was grateful to him for finding the perfect way to lift her spirits. "I'm guessing no one else knows that, though."

Clouds blew through his eyes, and he frowned as if her words pained him. Just as quickly as they'd appeared, they evaporated, leaving behind his customarily open expression. "Probably not. So, what're you up to tonight?"

Heather followed his lead and switched topics. "Absolutely nothing. I haven't had a chance to explore the town yet. Do you have any suggestions?"

"Downtown folds up like a tent at six, and this is the only thing open after that. There's a movie theater and mall over in Rockville, but that's a half hour away."

Heather wrinkled her nose. An hour-long

round-trip for things that she wasn't remotely interested in doing sounded more like self-imposed torture than fun to her. Then inspiration struck, and she asked, "Are you busy?"

"Not hardly. What'd you have in mind?"

"I promised to give you a waltzing lesson. How about now?"

"Sounds good." When the waitress dropped off the check, Heather reached into her bag for her wallet, but he waved her off. "It's on me."

"But you weren't planning on company. At least let me get the tip."

"Not a chance. I'm a Southern boy, and we don't let a lady chip in for her own dinner. I'd sooner work in the kitchen to pay Cam, and I hate washing dishes."

As he stood to pull out her chair for her, she wasn't sure what to make of his sudden flare of stubbornness. She'd gotten accustomed to his laid-back personality, so his adamant refusal caught her by surprise. In a good way.

"All right, then," she finally agreed, smiling over her shoulder at him. "Thank you."

"Anytime."

Chapter Seven

The Closed sign was on the door when Josh and Heather walked into Pampered Paws. Erin looked over from where she was hanging brightly colored puppy collars on a half-empty rack. Disapproval flashed in her eyes, but she quickly masked it with a smile for Heather. "Hey there. What're you guys up to?"

It didn't take a genius to figure out that her thinly veiled suspicion was aimed at him, but since she hadn't addressed him by name, Josh chose to ignore it and just grinned. He'd been tormenting his big sister since he'd first come to understand the concept, and he was well aware that she hated it when he pretended to be clueless. Almost as much as when he actually was clueless.

"Josh bought me dinner over at the Oaks Café," Heather explained. "So I'm returning the favor with a dancing lesson. I know you'll be down here working on inventory, so we'll try to keep the noise to a minimum."

"Speaking of dancing," Erin said, crossing the floor to pick up a sheet from the counter, "six more bidders registered for the bachelor auction today. That brings us up to forty, and the event isn't till the end of May."

Heather's eyes shimmered with excitement. "That's fabulous! Fifty was our goal, and we might end up with even more. If these ladies are feeling extra generous, maybe we'll be able to afford to replace those ruined picnic tables, too."

Erin gave him a long look before saying, "You didn't tell her?"

"It was gonna be a surprise," Josh replied, trying to imitate Mike's growl but failing completely. Since it wasn't his style to be gruff, he shrugged it off with a grin. "I'm building the tables myself out of some scrap lumber Cam had lying around after the Oaks Café's renovation. That way, we'll have plenty of spots for people to sit and it won't cost anyone a dime."

"Really?" He nodded, and Heather shook her head. "Between the farm and the playground, where are you going to find time for building tables?"

He enjoyed pitching in when he could, and

folks around town were used to him lending a hand on various projects during the year. They didn't think anything of it, so her praise was new to him. Feeling awkward, he answered, "I like keeping busy. Besides, there's always time for the really important stuff."

"Like waltzing lessons?"

"Well, now, that's a whole different deal, isn't it? Ya gotta have fun once in a while."

Heather rewarded him with the kind of dazzling smile that could go to a guy's head if he wasn't careful. "You think dancing with me will be fun?"

In all honesty, he'd been looking forward to it ever since she'd first suggested it. But with Erin staring at him as if he were a potential shoplifter, he decided it was best to play it cool. "Long as I don't crush your toes or spin you down the stairs, it should go just fine."

She laughed and headed for the door that led upstairs to her apartment. As he turned to go, Erin announced, "I need a tall guy to help me with something down here, Heather. I'll send your student up when he's done."

"Sounds good. I'll go put on my steel-toed pumps."

Flashing a sassy look over her shoulder at him, she turned and continued up the steps.

He was still watching her when Erin's palm

smacked the back of his head. "Hey! What was that for?"

"I warned you, Joshua," she hissed, using his full name as if that would make more of an impact than her hand. "What on earth are you thinking?"

"I'm thinking you want me to sell some poor, unsuspecting woman a ticket for something I can't do. Heather offered to give me some pointers so I don't make a total fool of myself, and I figured it made sense to take her up on it."

Doubt crept into his sister's gaze, and she narrowed her eyes at him. "The dance auction wasn't my idea. It was Heather's. And while we're on the subject, what possessed you to say yes in the first place?"

He was getting annoyed with everyone second-guessing his motives, and he let that irritation into his voice. "I'm doing it for the kids, so we can finish the playground before Parker, Abby and Bailey graduate from high school."

The moment he said it, he knew he'd made a terrible—and telling—slip by including Bailey in his list. And judging by Erin's suddenly compassionate expression, she'd heard it loud and clear. "You really like Heather, don't you?"

"What's not to like?" he said as casually as

he could manage. "She's smart and pretty, and she laughs at my jokes."

"Besides which, you love kids, and her niece already thinks you're Superman." He didn't know how to respond to that, so he kept quiet. She studied him for several moments, and his big sister's laser-focus appraisal made him want to squirm. He managed not to give in to the impulse, but it wasn't easy.

"Josh, I know that you want what Mike and Drew have," Erin went on in a gentler tone, "how important family is to you. But these two aren't ready for that yet. I'd hate to see you set your heart on someone whose life isn't in the same place as yours."

"Like Cindy, you mean," he added grimly.

"That girl broke your heart, not to mention your bank account."

"The jeweler took the ring back," Josh reminded her, grimacing at the humiliating memory. "I think he felt sorry for me."

"But that didn't help mend anything inside you. It took you a long time to get over Cindy, and I don't want to see that happen again." Leaning closer, she murmured, "Don't tell Mike or Drew, but out of the three of you clowns, you're my favorite. For a boy, you're actually not half-bad."

"Thanks." Deciding it was time to bring

the mood back up, he winked. "I'll be sure to remind you of that when you're doing your Christmas shopping."

"And there's the maddening other half," she shot back, aggravation replacing the fond look she'd been wearing a second ago. Sighing in frustration, she gazed up at him with a pitying expression. "I can't tell you what to do, but promise me you'll be careful. For your sake, and for the Fitzgeralds'. They've been through enough this year."

Her unsolicited advice echoed what Mike had said to him during their lunch at the farm. Josh wasn't sure what she thought could go wrong, but she meant well, so he did his best to view her comment the way she'd intended. "I appreciate your watching out for me, sis. You're not half-bad yourself."

He moved past her, stopping just long enough to drop a kiss on her cheek.

"Oh, you're a real piece of work, Kinley boy," she scolded him through a proud smile. "Now, get outta here before I change my mind."

"Yes, ma'am."

Grinning, he took the creaky steps three at a time on his way up to Heather's apartment. When he stepped into her living room, he was impressed by the transformation. Last time he'd been here, the place had been full of boxes and furniture stacked with suitcases. Now, there were bright throw pillows scattered around and floor-length curtains on the windows, giving the small space a nice, cozy feeling. Family photos crowded one of the built-in bookshelves, and he went over to check them out.

"I didn't have room for all of them," Heather told him from the kitchen, "so I let Bailey pick her favorites."

One in particular caught his eye, and he lifted the frame for a better look. A young couple sat together in a hospital bed, a tiny baby held between them. They looked tired but content, with no idea that in a few short years, their daughter would be an orphan. So much promise in the little family, Josh mused, only to end in sorrow. He wasn't usually one for brooding, and that thought made him sadder than he'd been since losing his own father years ago.

Heather joined him in the living room, and he hunted for something positive to say. "They look happy."

"They were." With a wistful smile, she took the frame from him and set it back in its place. "I was away at college, and they called me around midnight to tell me Polly had gone into labor early. I drove like a crazy woman to get there in time, and I made it to the delivery room just before Bailey was born. This was the best day of all our lives. So much has happened since then, it seems like a lifetime ago."

"Bailey's blessed to have an aunt who loves her the way you do." When Heather gave him a quizzical look, he tried again. "You've given up a lot for her, from that night right up till now. I'm sure you get plenty of offers for jobs that pay way better than this one, but you came here for Bailey. It can't be easy to make that work, but you're doing it."

Heather stared up at him, slowly shaking her head. "How on earth could you know that? I got one from a place in Louisville the other day, but I didn't tell anyone about it."

"Common sense," he replied with a shrug. "You're really good at what you do, so it'd be crazy to believe you didn't have other options. Maybe even some that didn't include living in a tiny apartment above your boss's pet store."

"The rent fits into my budget, so I'm not complaining."

He got the feeling that she wanted to tell him something more but wasn't sure whether or not she could rely on him to keep it to himself. He'd learned over the years that the best way to get someone's trust wasn't to ask for it, but to earn it. Whether you were talking about animals or people, gaining their confidence took a considerable amount of patience. But in the end, that was the best approach, and he chose it now.

"So," he began, rubbing his hands together as if he couldn't wait to get started, "the waltz. What do we do first?"

"Music." Going over to the mini speaker system on the windowsill, she plugged in her phone and scrolled through the list of songs. "I'm thinking this will work for starters."

The room filled with the highbrow chords of a full orchestra, and he couldn't help laughing. "I feel like I'm way underdressed."

"You're fine. Now, you put your left hand here—" she guided his hand to rest on her waist "—and take my right hand lightly in yours. This isn't the tango, so you won't be flinging me around. A nice, loose hold is what we're after."

Josh was a lifelong farmer, more at home with picks and shovels than white gloves. Doing his best to follow her instructions, he asked, "Is this okay?"

"Yes, but you need to relax your posture a little. More fluid, so your steps will be smoother."

After several attempts, each one clumsier

than the last, she stepped back and gave him an odd look. "Are you okay? It feels like you're made of wood or something."

"I told you, I don't dance," he reminded her curtly. "This is why."

"You plowed through a falling-down building to rescue a little girl. This should be a piece of cake for you."

"I'm trying."

"Yes, you are," she snapped, sounding as frustrated as he felt. Pinching the bridge of her nose, she thought for a minute and then said, "Let's go at this another way. Close your eyes."

"Why?"

"Because I said so. Honestly, Josh, you're twice my size. What do you think I'm going to do to you?"

She had a point there, he had to admit. But he was a hands-on kind of guy, so this cerebral approach to dancing was an uncomfortable stretch for him. "Okay, but if you tell me to picture us floating around on a cloud or something, I'm outta here."

Giving him a chiding look, she rolled those gorgeous baby blues. "Duly noted. Now close your eyes."

When he did, she took his hands and put them back in place, shaking his right one slightly. "Just let your fingers open up. It's ballroom dancing, not football."

He laughed, and she guided him through a few exercises that had him feeling much more flexible than he had at the beginning of their lesson.

"That's great," she said proudly. "Keep going, but open your eyes."

He did as she'd asked and realized that they were following the music. Slowly, but smoothly and without inflicting bodily injury on either of them. Grinning down at her, he asked, "Is it my imagination, or are we dancing?"

"Waltzing, actually. Very well, I might add. Once you relax, you're an excellent student."

"Well, I have a great teacher."

She thanked him, but he couldn't help noticing that there was more than appreciation twinkling in those beautiful eyes. Inspired, he reeled her in a bit, giving her a chance to pull away if she wanted to.

She didn't, and before he knew what he was doing, he'd leaned in to brush his lips over hers. They curved into a smile, and he lingered for a much longer kiss. He relished the sensation of holding her in his arms, her soft curves melting against him with a trusting sweetness that made him feel humble and amazing all at once.

Reluctantly, he broke the connection with her and took her hands as he stepped away. "I should get going."

"What? Why?"

"This is a real small town," he explained patiently, brushing a stray curl back from her cheek. "Folks saw us together at dinner, and they saw me come in here with you. If I stay much longer, they're gonna assume the worst. Then they'll start talking, and you might not like what they have to say about you. And I don't think you'd want Bailey hearing it, either."

"But it won't be true."

"In my experience, gossips aren't big on checking their facts before passing them along."

"You're totally serious about this, aren't you?" When he nodded, she blew out an aggravated breath. "Maybe small-town life isn't for me, after all."

"Aw, it's not so bad. Folks also know when you're in trouble and come to help you out, just like you'd do for them if they needed you."

"You've got a point there. I lived in my Detroit apartment for three years and didn't even know my neighbors' names," she conceded in a gentler voice.

Her quick turnaround sparked a flare of

hope inside him. Was it possible that this city girl might find a way to be happy in his hometown? Much as he hated to admit it, the thought of her moving away to take one of those other, higher-paying jobs really bothered him. Having been left behind by an ambitious woman before, he wasn't keen on setting himself up for a repeat performance.

Heather was so committed to building a solid foundation for Bailey, he suspected that once the girl started kindergarten, the lovely Fitzgerald ladies would be staying put until she graduated from high school. He could only hope that they chose to put down those roots in Oaks Crossing.

And if they did, he'd be there. Every day, in every way that he could manage. Because somewhere along the line, he'd started falling for this beautiful, challenging woman and her adorable niece. They'd make some man a wonderful family.

Despite his efforts to keep his distance, he could no longer deny that the more time he spent with them, the more he wanted that man to be him.

Sunday morning dawned sunny and warm. In the tree outside Heather's bedroom window, birds were calling to each other from the branches. Their bright chirping was a perfect accompaniment to the scent of fresh gourmet coffee wafting in from the new programmable coffeemaker her parents had sent her as a housewarming gift. Moving carefully to avoid waking Annabelle, she padded down the hall in her bare feet to pour herself a cup of rich, genuine French coffee.

Quiet mornings were rare for her, and she wandered over to the bay window to see what was going on outside. Two elderly couples had just met on the sidewalk in front of the building, exchanging handshakes and hugs before going into the Oaks Café for breakfast. Other people were scattered around, walking dogs in the park or driving down Main Street on their way somewhere.

It was as if the town itself was yawning and slowly waking up to face the day. The comment she'd made last night about small-town life not being for her echoed in her memory, and she reconsidered that while she sipped her coffee. Granted, there wasn't much going on here after dinnertime, but that gave people a chance to spend time with their families or hang out with their friends.

Like Josh Kinley.

Just the thought of him made her smile. Somehow, the tall country boy managed to be easygoing and charming, all while making her feel like the most fascinating woman he'd ever met. Registrations for the bachelor dance auction had come in at a snail's pace until word had gotten around that a dance with him was up for grabs, and sign-ups had doubled. Clearly, he could spend his precious spare time with any woman who lived within ten miles of Oaks Crossing.

But for some reason, he'd chosen to devote an entire evening to her. Recalling their first kiss, she couldn't hold back a romantic sigh. The feeling of those strong arms wrapped around her had stayed with her long after he'd left, following her into her dreams. That kind of thing never happened to her, and while she didn't understand what was going on between them, one thing was obvious.

There was something more between Josh and her than the simple friendship she'd planned on. The question was: Did she want that?

Curling up in the window seat, she rested her head against the glass and let her mind wander back through the eventful weeks since her arrival in Oaks Crossing. Ever since that first day when he'd stepped forward to help a total stranger, he'd been there for her when she needed him. And Bailey, too. The little girl adored him, looking up to him in a way Heather could never have anticipated.

Kind and generous, ready to stand between her and disaster, he was the sort of guy she'd always assumed lived only between the covers of a sappy romance novel. That someone like Josh Kinley existed in the real world was amazing enough. That she'd found him here in this sleepy Bluegrass town was almost more than her logical mind could accept.

Her cell phone rang from its stand, and she glanced over to see Joanna Simon's name on the caller ID. Immediately jumping to the assumption that it was bad news, her heart leaped into her throat and she took a breath to steady her voice before answering. "Good morning. How are things going over there?"

"Couldn't be better," her new friend assured her. "The girls are having a wonderful time, and they asked if Bailey could stay longer. I was wondering if you'd allow her to come to church with us."

Now that she knew nothing was wrong, Heather couldn't help feeling that some divine influence was at work here, nudging her back to the faith that she'd abandoned in favor of sleeping in on Sundays. Deciding that it could do them both good to attend a church service, she said, "I think she'd really enjoy that. In fact, I'm planning on going myself."

"Wonderful! We'll bring Bailey's things with us and hand her back to you afterward."

"I'll see you later, then."

"We're looking forward to it. Goodbye."

After they hung up, Heather showered and dressed in record time. In the back of her closet she found a dress that she hadn't worn in forever but had held on to because it was too pretty to give up. Covered in tiny multicolored flowers with a narrow line of lace at the modest neckline, it seemed appropriate for the occasion. After drying her hair, she smoothed it back with a velvet headband and stepped into ballet flats, then pirouetted in front of the mirror to assess her reflection.

Totally country, she decided with a smile. Perfect.

Feeling lighter than she had in months, she all but skipped down the stairs and out the front door. On the sidewalk, she was surprised to find plenty of other people wearing nice clothes and headed in the same direction she was. Several of them recognized her and greeted her warmly, introducing her to their companions. By the time she reached the old-fashioned white chapel at the end of the street, she felt like one of the locals.

She'd been to the building many times, but always when she was shuttling Bailey to the temporary day care that had been set up in the basement. Her first visit to the main area had been during the storm, and she'd been so terrified, she hadn't noticed much about it. It was sturdily built, and the timbers inside were aged oak, probably from some of the trees that had given the town its picturesque name. She paused in the entryway, peering through the open doors to see if there was a place for her to sit near the back.

"Morning, sunshine." A familiar voice drawled from behind her.

Angling a look over her shoulder, she smiled up at Josh. "Good morning to you, too. What did I do to earn such a nice greeting?"

"Showed up in that dress."

"It's a lot different from what I usually wear."

"Yeah." He gave her a quick once-over, admiration twinkling in his eyes. "I like it better."

"Really? I'll have to remember that." What on earth was wrong with her? she groaned silently. She was in a church, and here she was flirting with him like a love-struck teenager. Hoping to regain some of her dignity, she said, "I guess we should go in and find a place to sit."

"Ladies first," he said, motioning her ahead of him.

"You know," she commented as they walked in, "your Southern gentleman routine is starting to grow on me."

"I'm glad to hear that."

"Aunt Heather!"

She turned at the sound of Bailey's voice and saw her niece waving from her seat on the aisle. She was wearing a blue dress that she must have borrowed from Cara and a big, delighted smile. It struck Heather that she hadn't seen it since the last time she'd visited them before Craig died. Grateful tears stung her eyes, and she blinked them away as she leaned down to hug her niece. "Hey there, bean. I heard you had fun with the Simons last night."

"It was awesome." Sliding over, she patted the bench beside her. "Cara and I saw you come in, so we saved seats for you and Josh."

You and Josh? Heather echoed silently. Bailey couldn't possibly know about their cozy dance lesson, and Heather wondered where the girl had gotten the idea that she and Josh were now a pair. Hoping to sound nonchalant, she said, "That was thoughtful of you, but I think Josh would probably rather sit with his own family."

She glanced up at him, and he met her concern with a grin. "Looks like there's room for two on the end here, long as Bailey doesn't mind sharing her hymnal with us."

In response, the girl held up her book and handed it to him. *Outfoxed by a preschooler*, Heather groused silently as she took her seat.

The congregation's singing was enthusiastic and remarkably in tune, led by Mrs. Wheaton on the organ and a small but robust chorus up front. When the last chord faded, Cara stood up and whispered, "Please excuse us. It's time for Sunday school."

To Heather's surprise, Bailey followed Cara without hesitation, mixing in with the line of children following Lily Kinley and another young woman out of the chapel and downstairs.

"She'll be fine," Josh murmured without looking at her. "Lily and Abby will keep an eye on her for you."

His assurance eased her concern, and Heather realized that it hadn't taken her long to feel comfortable relying on her boss's family for the kind of support she'd been missing before coming to Oaks Crossing. She was accustomed to counting on herself for everything, and the difference was a welcome change from the nearly anonymous existence she'd known in Michigan. It was her home state, and she couldn't help feeling that she should have more of an attachment to it. But with her parents traveling full-time and her brother gone, there had been nothing keeping her in Detroit other than a job and her memories. The first she'd replaced easily enough, and the other she would always carry with her, no matter where she might find herself living in the future.

When it occurred to her that the pastor was speaking, she jerked her mind out of the past and turned her attention to the sermon. Middle-aged and modestly dressed, Pastor Wheaton could have passed for anyone's mellow grandfather as he surveyed the gathering with eyes that crinkled when he smiled. Which, judging by the lines at the corners, he did quite a bit.

Unhurried and filled with genuine emotion, his sermon about the importance of family was pleasant but unremarkable. For Heather, the bigger impact of it came from sneaking glimpses of the congregation's reactions to his words. People nodded in agreement or frowned when they apparently recognized themselves in the story. And then, one line snared her, and she stared at him in amazement.

"Family encompasses more than just the clan we're born into," he said in a gentle tone laced with understanding. "For many of us, it includes the people we come across who reach out to us and make a place for us in their hearts. Their generosity of spirit and selfless desire to help us reach our full potential make them a huge part of who we strive to become. Related or not, it's these gracious souls who lead us to where God wants us to go, so that we can become all He intends for us to be."

The preacher couldn't have summed up Heather's earlier thoughts any better if he'd tried. Impressed by his knack for connecting with his flock in such a personal way, she leaned toward Josh and whispered, "He's really good."

"You should hear him sing karaoke."

She smothered a laugh, and Josh winked at her as if they were two kids sharing a secret in church, rather than adults who should have known better. She'd been so serious for so long, the mischievous country boy was like a breath of fresh air to her. One she didn't even realize she needed until he blew into her life and showed her that there was so much more to enjoy.

"And now," Pastor Wheaton announced, holding his arms out like the showman he obviously was, "our Sunday-schoolers have a treat for us."

The kids who had left earlier trouped back into the sanctuary, and Heather was astonished to hear the worshippers applauding. As if that weren't enough, people were calling out to their children as they went past, waving and snapping photos. Once they'd assembled in front of the congregation, Lily waited for them to settle. As a kindergarten teacher, she'd clearly learned a great deal about handling children, and she didn't have to do anything more than fold her hands and look at them to quiet them down.

Heather made a mental note to ask Lily how she managed to command respect from such an unruly bunch, then sat back to listen. Delivered in fragile voices that wandered through the soprano range, it was the most adorable version of "Jesus Loves Me" that she'd ever heard. Even more important to her, though, was the joy illuminating Bailey's face while she sang. Standing beside her new friend, she no longer had the look of someone whose entire world had come crashing in on her a few months ago.

The pastor's words about finding family along your path came back to her, and she sent up a silent prayer of thanks for Erin and all the

Kinleys. They'd made a place for her and Bailey in the raucous circle of their family, and she knew there was no way she could ever thank them enough for their kindness.

But she could certainly try.

When the service was over, people hung back to talk with each other, many of them making plans together for the rest of the day. Several men were discussing the work to be done at the playground, and one of them got Josh's attention to ask if he and his brothers were coming.

"We wouldn't miss it," he assured them.

"Mostly 'cause the Reds aren't playing till tonight, right?"

Josh grinned, and they all laughed as they got back to hammering out the details for their work crew.

"Do you ever take an afternoon off?" Heather asked him.

"Sure. When it rains."

"Any other time?" she prodded as they blended into the crowd heading for the exit.

Looking up at the beamed ceiling, he made a show of considering her question before shaking his head. "I get bored if I don't have anything to do. It took me a few years to get that old cottage up to speed, and now that it's done I'm always looking for a project. I'm not crazy about the reason for it, but working on the playground will actually be a nice distraction from driving a tractor up one row and down the other."

"Did you ever think of doing something else? Besides farming, I mean," she clarified when he gave her a quizzical look.

"Why?"

Blunt and to the point, the response was so Josh, she couldn't help laughing. "That's my answer, I guess. I can't recall ever meeting someone so content with where they are and what they do."

"Well, now you have," he replied, adding a slow grin for good measure. They stopped near the Simons' car so Bailey could get her overnight things from the trunk. "Were you and Bailey planning to come out to the farm for lunch today?"

"Were we invited?"

"Always."

For some reason, the way he said it made her smile. He was tough to resist, this laid-back farmer with the big heart and the devastating grin. "Then we'll be there."

"Awesome. See you then."

After flashing her another warm smile, he flipped Bailey's ponytail before sauntering over to his truck.

"He likes you, Aunt Heather," Bailey commented innocently, gazing up at her with hope shining in her blue eyes. "Do you like him, too?"

Who wouldn't? Heather nearly blurted before she caught herself. Feeling the Simons' curious eyes on her, she knew her cheeks were starting to pink with embarrassment. To cover her reaction, she slung the backpack onto her shoulder. "Thanks again for having Bailey over last night, Joanna. I can see she had a wonderful time."

"You're welcome anytime, Bailey," Joanna said, her husband nodding his agreement. "Enjoy the rest of your Sunday."

"Bye, Bailey," Cara said, waving over her shoulder. "See you at day care tomorrow."

Taking Bailey's hand, Heather guided her onto the sidewalk that led home.

"You know what I like best about Oaks Crossing?" Bailey asked as they strolled along.

"What's that?"

"Everyone here feels like a family, even if they're not."

The artless comment summed up what Heather had noticed during church, and she put an arm around her niece for a quick hug. "I like that, too."

"I was scared about it at first, but I'm really glad we moved here. I have lots of friends now, and I love Sunday school. I never want to leave."

"Me, neither."

Surprised to hear her own response, Heather examined the instinctive answer for a moment, searching for a flaw she never found. For the first time in her adult life, she'd allowed her heart to speak for her, and staying here was what it wanted. The trick, she knew, was to find a way to do that without going bankrupt.

Unfortunately, that would be easier said than done.

Chapter Eight

"Okay, right there," Frank, their voluntary contractor, ordered, eyes fixed to the level he held upright on the beam Josh was helping to bolt in place. "Don't move."

"Gotcha."

Since he was stranded in his current position for the next few minutes, he took the opportunity to appreciate the improvements that had gone on at the playground since the storm. All the debris had been hauled away, and what remained had been inspected and approved for continued use. Across the square, repairs to the day care center were almost finished, and if you hadn't seen it beforehand, you'd never have guessed that a section of the house had collapsed under a fallen tree.

That was good, because every time he'd driven past it, recalling how close they'd come to a tragedy, that knowledge had sent a chill up his spine. He could only imagine how Heather and Bailey felt, going past the place every morning on their way to day care at the church. Josh understood how it felt to lose someone important to him, and how the life-changing experience made you cling even tighter to the family you had left. The Fitzgeralds only had each other, which made their connection all the more precious to them.

Again, he silently thanked God for intervening on that awful day. Heather might act calm and in charge most of the time, but he'd glimpsed a sliver of her vulnerable side and how deeply she cared for the things that were important to her. She'd uprooted her entire life and detoured her career plans for the sake of Bailey's happiness. Anyone who sacrificed so much for a child who wasn't her own deserved to get some help from above every once in a while.

"That's good for now, Josh," Frank told him, adding a tired sigh. "Let's take five."

"Are you okay?"

"Up all night with a colicky baby is all," he replied with a wan smile. "Nothing a day off won't cure."

"Except for the fact that this time of year you get as many days off as I do." To emphasize his point, Josh held his thumb and forefinger up in a big zero.

"It's supposed to rain on Wednesday," the builder commented in a hopeful voice.

That wasn't the forecast Josh had heard, but he hated to ruin the guy's day, so he kept his weather report to himself. "The repair committee's got a snack table over there, so I'm gonna get something to eat. Can I bring you anything?"

"Coffee, black," he groaned, sinking down to sit with his back against a tree. Before Josh had taken two steps, Frank's eyes were closed.

If the poor man's sleepless night was typical for fathers, Josh was gladder than ever that he had his own place and no longer lived in the Kinley farmhouse. Especially now that Mike and Lily were expecting a little one of their own. Doing his laundry there was convenient, and he loved seeing his family at meals, but at the end of a long day, he treasured the peace and quiet of his cottage in the woods. At this point in his life, he preferred being fun Uncle Josh to fatherhood.

Drew had once felt the same way, Josh mused as he waited in line at the sandwich table. But now, he was excited to have a child who, in his own words, would be the best of Bekah and him in one cute package. It was as if a switch had flipped inside him, changing his perspective on what meant the most to him.

Was that how it worked? Josh wondered. He loved kids, had a blast horsing around and teasing them, but he'd never officially been responsible for anyone but himself. Did you have to grow up enough to hit that phase of your life, or was there something else that made you feel ready to be someone's dad?

The person in front of him stepped to the side, and Josh saw Heather standing on the opposite side of the table, rearranging sandwiches whose waxed paper wrappers were labeled in her neat handwriting.

Figuring that God had just given him an answer to his question, Josh couldn't help grinning. "Hey there."

She looked up and nearly knocked him over with the dazzling smile he knew he'd never get tired of seeing. "Hey yourself. How's it going over there?"

"Good, but Frank needed a break so I came to get him some coffee. Better make it a large."

"And you're starving." When he grinned again, she shook her head with an indulgent smile. "As usual. Help yourself, and I'll get your friend some fresh caffeine."

"Thanks."

While he waited, Josh took a cup of lemonade and stacked ham and roast beef sandwiches on top. Then he added a couple of chocolate chip cookies for good measure.

When Heather returned, she eyed him doubtfully. "Would you like a hand carrying all this?"

Josh hadn't originally intended to take so much, but since he had, he figured it wouldn't hurt to have some help to make sure it all got to where it was going in one piece. "That'd be great. Everything looks so good, I couldn't resist."

"And you're starving," she repeated with a knowing look.

"Yeah, that, too."

She laughed, and as they strolled across the park, she said, "Things are looking really nice over at the day care. Tammy told me they're planning to be back in by June first."

"That's good to hear. Bailey must be happy."

"Actually, she really likes going to the church. She said it feels like someone's watching over them there."

"That's 'cause someone is," Josh commented. "But God was keeping an eye on her at the center, too, so you could try reminding her of that. He's all around, not just at church."

Heather stopped in midstride and stared up at him with a pensive expression. He wondered if he'd crossed some kind of line with her, but then—thankfully—she smiled. "I was thinking the exact same thing during the service this morning, when I saw how much everyone seems to enjoy being there. It seemed as if they were there for more than just the sermon, or so the neighbors would give them credit for showing up. So many people I've known act like God is taking attendance and that being in a pew on Sunday covers whatever bad things they do during the week."

No wonder she didn't think church was important, he thought wryly. If you were surrounded by people who viewed it as some kind of roll call, it would be impossible for you to understand the importance of having faith. Not to mention sharing it with others.

"Well, folks around here don't care much for appearances. Pretty as you are, what you do means a lot more to us than how you look."

"You know," she confided in a shy voice, "when we first met, I thought you were being nice to me to get on my good side."

"I was," he assured her with a grin.

"But now that we've gotten better acquainted," she continued in her serious mode, turning to face him so he'd know she meant business, "I've seen for myself that you're like that with everyone. You really are one of the good guys, Josh. There aren't many of you left."

The affection sparkling in her eyes pulled him in, and he didn't even bother trying to joke it away. Instead, he slid his arms around her, drawing her close enough to make it clear what he was feeling, but not close enough to cause a scandal that would give his mother apoplexy. "What makes you say that?"

"Trust me, I've looked. A lot." Settling her hands on his shoulders, she asked, "How about you?"

"The same." Holding her in his arms felt so right, he could easily picture doing it for the rest of the afternoon. And so, he pushed off the last of his doubts and jumped. "But I think I'm done hunting now."

A spark of surprise lit her face, and a pretty blush crept over her cheeks. "Really?"

"Uh-huh."

"Me? But I'm so demanding and always talking, and I'm never satisfied with anything the way it is."

"You really need to take some marketing lessons from Bekah," he teased. "You make yourself sound like the wicked witch and evil queen all rolled into one gorgeous package."

"You like all that?" He nodded, and he could

see her wavering. Then, in a heartbeat, the hopeful look clouded over. "What about Bailey?"

"She's terrific. In case you haven't noticed, I love kids."

"I noticed, but I wasn't sure how you'd feel about getting involved with someone who has so many responsibilities."

"It's not the way I expected my life to be going right now, but that doesn't mean it's a problem. Just 'cause things are different from what I imagined doesn't mean they're worse. They're just different." To drive his point home, he dropped in for a light kiss, then rested his chin on top of her head. "I didn't mean to spring this on you in the middle of the park. Hope you're okay with it."

"Oh, yeah," she said, cuddling against him with a little sigh. "I'm very okay with it."

Their private moment was briefer than he'd have liked. Bailey zoomed over from her post at the snack table, obviously excited about something.

"See, Aunt Heather?" she gloated, ponytail bouncing as she danced in place. "I told you Josh liked you."

"You did?" he asked. When she nodded eagerly, he laughed and held out an arm to draw her into their cozy circle. "Thanks, sweetness. I appreciate your putting in a good word for me."

"You're welcome. Abby and Parker were telling me about the parade on Memorial Day. Parker's marching with the band, and Abby's going to ride in a carriage with Mike and Lily. They invited me to go, too." Turning hopeful eyes on Heather, she added, "Can I? Please?"

At first, Heather looked baffled by the suggestion. Then her expression brightened, and she gave Josh a delighted smile. "Is this one of those places that celebrates Memorial Day the old-fashioned way?"

"I don't know about old-fashioned, but we have a parade, and a service to honor local soldiers. Then there's a big picnic here in the square for anyone who wants to come. While everyone's together, I'm planning to shanghai a few more volunteers for our playground work crew."

"You mean, you're going to show them how bad it is and shame them into helping with the repairs?"

"Whatever works," he said with a shrug. "It's harder to say no when you can see for yourself how much help we need to get this place up and running for the kids to use this summer."

"It's a great idea. It reminds me of how the rescue center holds those open houses to bring visitors in to meet the animals. Personalizing the issue makes people want to donate whatever they can spare."

"Sometimes folks want to help out, but they don't know how."

"It's like when Annabelle came to the center," Bailey chimed in. "We weren't looking for a kitten, but you saw her and knew she needed us to take care of her."

"Smart kid," Josh commented with a grin.

"Yes, she is."

She ran a gentle hand over Bailey's head in a gesture that reminded Josh of how his own mother had treated him as a child. For some women, that kind of loving touch seemed to be instinctive, and Josh found himself wondering if he could be the guy who eventually won the hearts of the Fitzgerald girls.

Because that man would be happy for the rest of his life.

Heather couldn't remember the last time she'd been to a parade.

Growing up, she'd watched the big Thanksgiving one on TV while Mom babysat the turkey and turned out pie after mouthwatering pie. It was still a tradition for Heather, but now that her parents had fully embraced their gypsy lifestyle, it wasn't quite the same. This past Thanksgiving she'd recorded the parade so she could watch it after her shift at the emergency animal clinic, where she'd signed up to work some extra hours so people with families could enjoy their holiday.

The Oaks Crossing Rescue Center was being staffed by a rotation of volunteers today, so here she was standing on the sidewalk in front of Pampered Paws, waiting for the festivities to get started. Surrounded by flag-toting people who were talking and laughing, it was easy to enjoy the bright, sunny day that promised nothing but relaxation and baskets full of Maggie's wonderful home-cooked food.

"Hey, you." Josh greeted her as he hurried over from wherever he'd been.

"Hey, yourself. I was beginning to think you ditched me."

"Not hardly. Mike needed a hand unloading the trailer at the starting line. He can handle the carriage or the horses by himself, but not both at the same time. Bailey was pretty jazzed about meeting Penny and Ginger, so I figured I should warn you—she's probably gonna start asking for a horse."

"I'm pretty sure my lease doesn't allow livestock," Heather commented wryly. "We'll have to be content with Annabelle for a while."

"If Bailey wants to hang out with some ponies, you can sign her up for the Gallimore

Riding School. Mike and Lily run it, and the kids have a blast."

Heather's budget was stretched pretty thin already, so she wasn't eager to take on any more expenses. As if he'd read her mind, Josh added, "Since you work for Erin, I'm sure they'd let Bailey take lessons there for free."

"That's very tempting, but I wouldn't feel right about taking advantage of them like that."

"Then she could do some barn work to earn her keep. I'd make sure I'm there so you wouldn't have to worry about her being around the horses by herself."

Stunned by his quick response, she turned to him with a little smile. "How is it you always have a solution to my problems? Whether it's stepping in when a moving van shows up early, rescuing my niece or helping her get some riding lessons that I'm sure she'd love, you seem to have all the answers."

"Well, now," he drawled, "I guess I just have a knack for being in the right place at the right time."

And for stepping up to do more than any girl had a right to expect, she thought. She wasn't sure exactly when it had happened, but she'd come to rely on this easygoing country boy being there for Bailey and her. Sometimes even when she didn't realize she needed his help.

Determined to make her own way, Heather wasn't too proud to admit that there were times when her independent streak made her life more difficult than it had to be. Sharing those burdens with someone hadn't been an option for her recently, because she didn't dare start leaning on someone, only to topple over when they finally decided they'd had enough and left. Not only would she not do that to herself, she couldn't bear the thought of Bailey suffering that kind of heartache.

The starter's horn blared, and Josh stepped behind her as strains of music drifted up Main Street. Dressed in uniforms that had been in style decades ago, the Oaks Crossing band marched up the street behind a colorful banner that had obviously been made by hand. They were mostly in step with each other, and the rousing tune they played got everyone cheering, snapping pictures and waving at their kids as they marched past.

"Is that Parker playing the drums?" she asked.

"Yeah, it's his first year, and he loves it. He's really good, so even though he's in fourth grade, they asked him to march with the band today. It gets kinda loud when he's practicing, so Cam built him a studio in the workshop behind their house."

Some parents would have insisted that he

choose a quieter instrument, she mused in admiration. Parker was blessed to have been adopted by two people who loved him enough to encourage his interests, however deafening they might be. Now that she'd identified someone in the group, she paid closer attention to the music. "There aren't many of them, but they have a nice, big sound."

"That's one way to put it," Josh agreed with a chuckle. "At the last concert, the kid playing the chimes went a little nuts, and the whole thing crashed on the floor of the stage. He stood there holding his mallets and just kept on pretending to play. It was hilarious."

"Oh, no," she groaned. "You didn't laugh at him, did you?"

Josh made a derisive sound, as if he was offended that she'd even suggest such a thing. "'Course not. Just about choked holding it back, though."

That was Josh, she thought fondly. Generous and kind, he'd do anything to avoid hurting someone's feelings. The blast of a fire truck siren right in front of her made her jump back in surprise.

Josh laughed. "And here I thought city girls were immune to noise."

"Not that kind of noise," she corrected him

as her pulse descended from the stratosphere. "I wasn't prepared for them to do that."

"Kids love it, so the drivers make sure to sound off every few yards or so."

There were two trucks, older vehicles that had clearly seen a lot of action. But they gleamed like red mirrors in the sunshine, making it plain that the volunteers who manned the department took a lot of pride in showing off their equipment. Behind them rolled at least a dozen tractors, some with antique steam engines and others that looked more modern. Then there was a group of farm kids towing wagons loaded down with small animals from rabbits to turtles.

Sierra walked with them, next to a dappled gray pony hauling a larger wagon draped in bunting and sporting a sign identical to the one that hung on the post outside the rescue center. The litter of kittens that had come in on Heather's first day was in one cage that had a sign perched on top proclaiming that they were READY TO BE LOVED. The other held a creature she'd never seen in person.

"So beautiful," she breathed, leaning forward for a better look. "When did the falcon come in?"

"This morning. Sierra told me he's got a broken wing, but our rehabber says he'll be good as new in a few weeks and they can release him."

"That's how I found the clinic in the first place," Heather confided while a gaggle of Boy Scouts marched past. "I was cruising around the site and found a video from when they did a hawk release. It was so incredible, Bailey and I must have watched it half a dozen times. I was really impressed, and I emailed Erin the next day about the job opening they had listed on the main page."

"And the rest is history," he finished with a grin. "I'm real glad you saw that clip. Otherwise, I never would've met you."

"That's quite a line, country boy."

"Actually, it's the honest truth."

The grin broadened, but it was nothing compared to the warmth in those vivid blue eyes. He didn't kiss her, but she felt as if he had.

Fortunately, the clopping sound of hooves drew her attention to the rear of the parade, where several kids rode on horseback in front of the elegant carriage she'd noticed during a visit to Gallimore Stables. Used for weddings—including the one at which Mike and Lily had met—its graceful lines gleamed in the sunshine, but not as much as the matched pair of copper-colored horses who seemed to be dancing down Main Street. One tossed her head, and the other nickered to the crowd in an equine greeting. To Heather, it looked as if Penny and Ginger were enjoying their star status to the fullest.

Mike sat in the driver's seat beside Maggie, reins held loosely in his capable hands. Behind them, Lily, Abby and Bailey were smiling and laughing, waving to the crowd as they trotted by. Charlie and Sarge were along for the ride, too, paws resting on the back of Mike's seat while they took in the view. The delight shining in her niece's eyes was all the confirmation Heather needed that extending their stay in this charming town was the right thing to do for both of them.

Heather watched them until the caravan turned a corner and disappeared onto a side street. When she turned, Josh cocked his head in a questioning manner.

"So," he began in a casual tone, "does that smile mean you like our old-fashioned tradition?"

"Very much."

He seemed to be on the verge of adding something else, and Heather held her breath waiting to hear what he'd say next.

Thankfully, he simply flashed her a bright smile and angled her toward the park as a lone bugler's somber tune summoned people for the memorial service. They found Bailey in the midst of the Kinley clan, proudly holding Sarge's leash while the old terrier snoozed with his chin resting on her pink sneaker.

Heather and Josh stepped up behind her, and she leaned back against them, secure as any child could possibly be. You'd never have guessed that she'd been orphaned and uprooted from her home only a few months ago. While Heather was proud to be a part of that, she recognized that the close-knit residents of their new home had played a significant role in Bailey's recovery.

The murmuring crowd quieted as a small color guard made its way in from the far side of the green. The Stars and Stripes came first, followed by soldiers who carried the flags of the units they were currently serving. Men took off their hats, and children copied their parents when they held their hands over their hearts to recite the Pledge of Allegiance.

Simple as it was, the ritual touched Heather in a way that made her feel humbled by the show of reverence for people who'd sacrificed everything to keep their country safe. As if that weren't enough, the band played "America the Beautiful," and then the song that represented each branch of the military. At the end, they launched into "The Star-Spangled

Banner," accompanied by the crowd heartily singing along.

Eyes wide, Bailey was transfixed by the patriotic display, and Heather had to admit she felt pretty awed herself. There were no fireworks, but the army chaplain with the booming voice had no trouble keeping everyone's attention through a short sermon that ended with a prayer.

"We ask You, Lord, to keep all of our soldiers in Your care wherever they find themselves. Let them know that we remain grateful for their service every single day and will keep them in our prayers until the last one of them returns. Amen."

Heather whispered a heartfelt "Amen," then listened as the bugler stood at the edge of the assembly and played taps. When he was finished, from off in the distance came the reply, a ghostly reminder of men and women who would never be coming home.

As the final note drifted off on the warm breeze, she was relieved to see that she wasn't the only one discreetly wiping a tear from her cheek. She didn't know anyone in the military personally, so she didn't often stop to think about how difficult that existence must be for them and their families. Somber as the lesson was, it was an important one.

When the ceremony was over, the Kinley crew gathered in the shade of one of the grand oak trees that populated the square. They spread blankets over the grass, and Maggie set out a feast that looked large enough to share with half the town. Fried chicken, ham, salads and four different kinds of pie covered the blankets, and when she was finally satisfied with the arrangements, she held out her arms and smiled at the eager faces surrounding her.

"All right, then. Let's eat."

From that point on, it was like any other family meal Heather had enjoyed at the farm, minus the long table and benches. The boys argued, the girls chatted and, following Abby's lead, Bailey snuck scraps from her paper plate to Sarge when she thought no one was looking.

"Something wrong?"

When she heard the concern in Josh's voice, Heather realized that she'd paused with a roll in one hand and a plastic knife full of butter in the other. Smiling at her own foolishness, she shook her head while she spread the butter. "I was just thinking how great this is, slowing down to enjoy the day. Last Memorial Day, I worked a double shift at the clinic and never even got outside until it was dark."

Chewing a mouthful of his mother's scrumptious cherry pie, Josh frowned. "I can't imagine being stuck indoors like that. I'd go bonkers."

"I almost did," she admitted ruefully. "I'm glad to have those days behind me, that's for sure."

"Would you do it again?"

"You mean become a vet?"

"Yeah. Knowing what you know now, would you still make the same choice?"

Coming from him, the question startled her. Up until now, she'd gotten the impression that Josh was a free spirit who didn't examine life—his own or others'—all that closely. "I've always loved animals, and helping them is very rewarding for me. So yes, I'd do it again. How about you? If you could do anything, would you still want to be a farmer?"

"I didn't pick that," he corrected her gently. "God did. He planted me where He knew I'd do the most good, and I'm happy with that."

In a way, Heather realized, He'd done the same with her. "He really knows what He's doing, doesn't He? Even if things don't always make sense to us at the time, eventually they do. We just have to hang in there until that happens."

"That's why they call it faith."

"We live by believing, not by seeing,"

Heather said, quoting one of the few Bible verses she recalled from childhood.

"Exactly." Sprawling out, he leaned back on his elbows and crossed one long leg over the other. "'Course, for a science-y girl like you, that's more of a stretch."

"It was," she admitted, adding a grateful smile. "And then I met you."

"Just bein' me."

That was more than enough for her, but Heather didn't think that this was the time or place for a deep, emotional conversation. Fortunately, Bailey skipped over and plopped down between them. "Miss Tammy just told me the day care center will be open again next Monday, and they're having a party for everyone. I can go back, right?"

"Absolutely," Heather replied, hugging her around the shoulders. "In fact, it's probably time to sign you up for preschool in the fall."

"Awesome! Cara will be there, too, so it'll be fun." Turning to Josh, she added, "Will you come to the party with us next Monday?"

"Wouldn't miss it, sweetness. Just tell me what time, and I'll be there."

While the two of them talked about future events, including the day care celebration, Heather hung back and listened with growing appreciation for the man who'd done so much for her niece. Bailey had opened up to him in a way she'd never done with anyone outside their family, and the timidity that had once so concerned Heather was a distant memory.

His promise to attend the reopening of the school with them echoed pleasantly in her mind, and she couldn't help smiling. Busy as he was, he hadn't hesitated for even a second because he'd known it would make Bailey happy.

If there was a kinder, more caring man on the planet than Josh Kinley, Heather would be well and truly amazed.

Chapter Nine

It was almost closing time at the clinic, and Heather was gathering her things so she could pick up Bailey from day care before they closed. Just as she was locking the front door, a minivan pulled into the lot.

The driver flashed the headlights to get her attention, and she noticed that the woman was motioning for Heather to wait. The pleading look on her face made it clear this was an emergency, and she braced herself for something awful as she walked over to the driver's open window. "May I help you?"

"I know you only treat strays, but my daughter's new puppy is very sick, and the nearest vet is half an hour away. I can see you're ready to leave, but I didn't know what else to do. Can you please help us?"

Heather peeked into the backseat, where a

young girl sat in her car seat, cradling a limp black Lab puppy against her. Tears had dried on her cheeks, and more were streaming down in a silent plea for someone to do something. Heather couldn't just leave if there was a way for her to help them, so she smiled. "Come on inside. I have to make a quick call, and then we'll see what's going on."

"Really?" the distraught mother asked, obviously relieved. "Thank you."

Heather unlocked the door while she debated what to do about Bailey. She didn't know how long she'd be, and while she knew Erin would pick up Bailey for her, she hated to drag her boss away from the pet store. Then inspiration struck, and she pulled up a now-familiar number. "Hi, Joanna? This is Heather. I hate to bug you, but there's an emergency here at the clinic, and I was hoping you might run back to day care and take Bailey home with you."

"I'm here now, so it's no trouble at all. Wednesday is casual night at our house, so we're having pizza and watching the new princess movie that just came out. Is that all right with you?"

"I'm jealous," Heather replied with a laugh. "I'll be there to pick her up as quickly as I can. If you'll hand your phone to Tammy, I'll approve your taking Bailey home. Thanks so much."

"You're very welcome. We'll have plenty to go around, so you can join us when you get here and tell us how things went."

"That's really generous of you."

"Don't even think twice about it," the gracious woman said. "We working parents have to stick together."

Working parents, Heather echoed with a smile. That's what she was now, and while she'd known that in a general sense, until recently the responsibility of it had terrified her. Now that she had a network of supportive friends, the whole thing was easier to manage. Not easy, but not impossible, either. She liked knowing that she and Bailey now had friends they could count on.

After approving the change in routine, she shut off her phone, donned her lab coat and got to work. As she joined her visitors in the exam room, she reminded herself that this child must be terrified and needed some encouragement. Smiling, she said, "Grown-ups call me Dr. Fitzgerald, but you can call me Heather. What's your name?"

"Kayla."

"I'm Virginia Frederickson," the mother added.

"It's nice to meet you both." To Kayla, she said, "Who's your cute little friend?"

"Sally. She's really, really sick."

Needing slightly more to go on, Heather glanced at Virginia for details.

"We got her from a shelter on Saturday," the woman explained. "And she seemed fine. But on Monday, she stopped eating and didn't want to do anything but sleep. When I got home from work today, she was still in her puppy bed where she was this morning. Our baby-sitter said Sally hadn't done anything all day but whimper."

A quick examination told Heather that the pup's breathing was shallow, and her pulse was in hummingbird range. After gently inserting a thermometer, it took only a few seconds to determine that Sally's temperature was much higher than it should be. She also squirmed in discomfort, which Heather took as an encouraging sign.

"You're okay, baby," she crooned, gently smoothing fur that should be soft but was brittle from dehydration. She addressed her comments to Kayla, keeping the explanation short and simple. "Sally has some bad germs that are making her act like this. I'm going to help her drink some water and then give her medicine that will kill those nasty germs. She has to take it for a few days, but she should be feeling much better by this time tomorrow."

"Will she start eating again?" the girl asked.

"Like a little horse," Heather assured her, turning her attention to Virginia. "If she's still not doing well when you get home tomorrow, call me and I'll meet you here to see what needs to be done."

"Oh, thank you," the woman breathed in relief. "This is our first pet, and it's been so awful the past couple of days."

"I completely understand. My niece and I adopted a kitten recently, and she'd be very upset if Annabelle was feeling this bad. Kayla, if you can hold Sally nice and still for me, I'll get her ready to go home."

She filled a large dropper with water and chose an antibiotic that was appropriate for the puppy's age and weight. While she worked, it occurred to Heather that there must be other families in town whose pets got sick and had to be driven to Rockville for care. To her relief, the Lab swallowed the water without much fuss and took the shot like a champ.

Heather gathered together the oral version of the antibiotic and some vitamin treats that would help boost the dog's immune system. After putting everything in a bag, she wrote down the dosage instructions and added them to the bag with one of her business cards. "My cell number's on here, along with the clinic's.

If you need me, don't hesitate to call anytime. I love animals, and it's my job to keep them healthy."

"Bless you, Dr. Fitzgerald," the young mother said, shaking both of her hands warmly. "I can't thank you enough for staying to take care of us."

The phrasing caught her off guard, and as she walked them out, she realized that she had indeed been caring for the family as well as their dog. Physicians referred to that extra bit of compassion as a bedside manner, and while that didn't apply to her patients, she decided that the concept was more or less the same.

Alone in the clinic again, she cleaned up the exam room, disinfecting the table and stowing her equipment before heading for her car. As she drove into town, the satisfaction she felt whenever she was able to help an ailing animal gradually led her back to an idea that had started brewing at the Memorial Day parade. It had seemed crazy at the time, but now...

On a whim, she hit the speed dial for Josh, expecting to get his voice mail. Instead, she heard, "What's up, Doc?"

"So funny," she chided, laughing in spite of herself. "Have you got a minute?"

"For you? Always."

The casual way he said it made her feel

all warm and fuzzy, and she suspected that it wouldn't take much for her to get used to feeling that way around him. "I had an idea, and I want to run it past you."

"Shoot."

Pulling onto the shoulder so she wouldn't be distracted, she relayed her interesting encounter at the clinic, then got down to the real reason for her call. "I've been considering taking some part-time work at that animal hospital in Rockville, but if I'm driving back and forth to work there, any money I make will get swallowed up by a sitter for Bailey. Do you think there's a way to set up a more formal veterinarian's office at the rescue center? That way, I could cover both places and not be gone as much."

"I'd imagine we could work something out. Cam's got his building designer's license, and I hate to brag but I built most of my place from the floor up. When I moved in there, it wasn't much more than an old storage shed with some questionable electric and plumbing."

The fact that he didn't even hesitate made her want to turn excited cartwheels, something she'd seldom done even as a child. She should have known that Josh would not only be on board, but would step up and do whatever he could to help her make it happen. That was the kind of guy he was, after all.

"I could arrange to pay Erin rent for the space," she went on excitedly. "The steady extra income would be nice for both of us, and along with your new corn crop, it might be just the thing to get the farm's finances back on track."

"That'd be awesome. Where do I sign?"

Laughing, she thanked him and hung up, then pulled back onto the road and headed for the Simons' house. A grateful client, new opportunity and pizza. She couldn't have asked for a better way to end her day.

"That's what you're wearing?"

When he heard the all-too-familiar sound of his big sister's disapproval, Josh looked over to find her glaring at him over a clipboard. Glancing down at his best jeans and newish T-shirt, he shrugged. "These are my good boots."

"Seriously?"

"Aw, come on," he said with a grin. "This is the kind of stuff I always wear unless I'm going to church. You're selling ladies a dance with me, not some fancy-pants lawyer in a suit and tie."

A couple of women carrying bidding paddles sashayed past, fanning themselves with their paddles and flashing him smiles on their way into the school gym. Decked out in streamers, balloons and a mirrored disco ball, the festive environment the committee had created reminded him of his junior prom. He'd had a stellar time that night, and he wouldn't mind if this one went the same way. In truth, he was kind of hoping that Heather would decide to bid on him. There wasn't a rule against it, which he knew because he'd checked. Since she was the one who'd taught him to waltz, he thought it would be cool to show her just how good a student he was.

But that wasn't up to him, Josh reminded himself as Erin finally shook her head and continued toward whatever important errand she'd been heading for when she intercepted him. Figuring he'd dodged a bullet in not being ordered to drive home and change, he strolled around to say hello to folks he didn't usually see much until fall. This time of year, he was normally buried up to his neck in work and didn't leave the farm very often.

Heather had changed that for him, giving him a reason to venture into town. And that wasn't all she'd done since he'd met her and her charming niece. They'd shown him a fresh view of the hometown he loved but had come to take for granted over the years. For Bailey, everything was a big adventure, and it was fun for him to see familiar things through her young eyes.

Her very pragmatic aunt was another story altogether. By turns sweet and prickly, Heather still baffled him as much as she fascinated him. But during the playground work session and Memorial Day parade, the three of them had almost felt like a family to Josh. Ever since then, he'd caught himself wondering more than once if the Fitzgerald girls felt the same way.

As if on cue, Heather appeared in one of the open doorways, talking with another bachelor the organizers had shanghaied for the event. When Josh noticed that she was wearing the dress he'd admired during the first church service they'd attended together, he couldn't keep back a grin. He'd mentioned more than once how much he liked it, and he suspected it wasn't a coincidence she'd chosen to wear it tonight.

Apparently, the guy she was talking to wasn't very interesting company, because her eyes were drifting around the crowd as if searching for a way out of their conversation. When they fell on Josh, he caught her "help me" message and sauntered over to bail her out.

"Hey there," he said casually. "I can see

you're real busy, but do you mind if I ask you a couple of questions about how this is gonna work?"

"Of course. Excuse me, Steven."

The guy responded with a quick smile that didn't hide his disappointment. Heather grabbed Josh's arm as they walked away and muttered, "Thanks for the rescue."

"Well, you looked kinda bored." Sneaking a peek back at the competition, he chuckled. "Let me guess—banker."

"Worse," she groaned softly. "Stockbroker. One who likes to brag about his alma mater and his toys."

"He's not from around here. Wonder where they found him?"

"He told me he's in town visiting his sister's family, and she volunteered him at the last minute. He thinks she's trying to get him to find a nice girl and settle down here."

"You sure did learn a lot about him in just a few minutes."

She stopped walking and stared up at him. "You're not jealous, are you?"

"'Course not. Just 'cause he went to some fancy school and drives a car that costs more than a lotta houses doesn't mean anything." *At least it shouldn't*, Josh added silently.

Glancing around, she stepped in and said, "Can you keep a secret?"

"Sure."

"I like tractors and old pickups better than sports cars."

She flashed him a dazzling smile that made his heart turn over in his chest, and he grinned down at her. "Are you gonna bid on me?"

"Do you want me to?"

The flirtatious tone made him chuckle. "I wouldn't complain if you won, that's for sure."

"Then I'll definitely think about it. For now, I have work to do, and you should go line up with the other guys so Erin can decide which order she prefers to have you all come out in."

"Y'know," he grumbled in mock irritation, "one of these days, I'm gonna go off the beam and tell her what to do instead of the other way around."

Heather laughed. "Please let me know when you're planning to do that. I'd love to be there to see it for myself."

"She's not all that tough. We boys just cave because it's easier than arguing with her for an hour over a job that'd take us half that long." After a moment's thought, he added, "Don't tell her I said that, though. She'll take it as a challenge to prove me wrong."

"Another deep, dark secret you want me to

keep?" Heather teased. "If I agree, what's in it for me?"

"I promise to give you a dance tonight, whether you're the top bidder or not. And that's a big deal, because this spinning around in the spotlight is really not my thing."

"What made you change your mind?"

"You."

The response popped out of his mouth before he took the time to think it through, and he anxiously waited to see her reaction to the very personal revelation. To his great relief, she beamed up at him as if he'd just granted her fondest wish. "Do you really mean that?"

"Yeah, I do."

"That's the sweetest thing any man has ever said to me. Thank you."

Rewarding him with a sunny smile, she headed back into the gym. As he went in the other direction toward the bachelors' staging area, Josh knew he was grinning like a fool, but he didn't much care. He was doing his part to get the kids' playground back in action so Abby, Parker and Bailey could enjoy it with their friends this summer. It wasn't costing him more than a few hours of his time, and all he had to do was be pleasant company to someone who was generous enough to donate her money to the cause. For someone who'd normally still be out in the fields working right now, an event like this was pretty easy duty.

And after he'd fulfilled his obligation to the committee, one way or another, he was spending the rest of this rare evening off with the most intriguing woman he'd ever met. Life didn't get any better than that.

"Can you believe it?" Erin asked, grinning proudly. "We're almost at our goal, and we've still got three guys waiting to be bid on. At this rate, we'll be able to add the climbing nets we couldn't afford last time."

"That's wonderful," Heather said, giving her a quick hug. "You put together a great committee for this, and they've done a fabulous job."

Glancing around, Erin leaned in to speak more quietly. "Speaking of fabulous jobs, I couldn't have asked for a better veterinarian. You're great with the pets and the people, and you're putting in extra time to get more familiar with the wild ones. I can't imagine anyone being a better fit for us."

Although her voice was muted, there was a current of excitement running through her tone, and Heather felt her heart skip a beat or two in response. Hoping she wouldn't come across as too eager, she opted for humor. "What are you trying not to tell me?"

"I know you're on the radar for some other, bigger clinics, but I hope you'll decide to extend your contract with us. I understand that money is a real issue for you, but I think if we all put our heads together, we can come up with something that works for all of us."

"Actually, earlier this week Josh and I were discussing a way to expand the clinic's services and increase revenue for all of us."

Heather quickly outlined their idea, thrilled to see Erin nodding in agreement. "Absolutely. We'll hammer out the details later, but count me in."

Out front, the emcee called for the next bachelor, and he brushed past them as Heather stood there in shocked silence. She prided herself on being hard to shake, but Erin's rapid agreement was something she hadn't dared to hope for. With their new arrangement, she'd be able to continue in the position she'd come to enjoy so much and also have the money she needed to rent a small house for Bailey and her.

And be with Josh.

Far from trivial, the last advantage sealed it for her, and she held out her hand. "Then it's a deal. On Monday, we can write up something more formal, and I'll let that clinic know that I've accepted an offer. The perfect one," she clarified with a smile. "Thank you, Erin. I really appreciate your confidence in me."

"I just hate breaking in new people," the generous woman told her as she focused on what was going on at the podium. "It's such a pain."

Heather laughed, and as the bidding progressed, it was all she could do to keep her composure. She couldn't wait to tell Bailey that her dream about them staying in Oaks Crossing had come true.

"And now," the emcee announced into her mic, "our last bachelor of the evening. I'm sure most of you know him, and I assume that many of you have heard his classic line, 'Aw, darlin', it's sweet of you to ask, but I don't dance.'" Her higher-pitched imitation of Josh's drawl was bang on, and everyone laughed. "So break out those checkbooks and take your best shot, ladies, because you don't know when—or if—you'll have this chance again. Josh Kinley!"

She stepped back, and he strolled out from behind the temporary wall beside her as the mostly female crowd went totally bananas. When the hostess motioned for him to make a full turn like a runway model, he gave her one of those lazy grins and slowly complied, much to the crowd's delight. Once the applause and catcalls had died down, the emcee said,

"All right, then. You've gotten a good look at him, so someone get us started."

Heather timed the fast-paced action, and in less than a minute, Josh had scored their record bid for the night. She was happy about that, but part of her longed to jump in and make sure that she was the one who won that dance. Unfortunately, the figure quickly rose beyond what she could spare, and she realized that she'd have to content herself with knowing that Bailey and her friends would enjoy the newly repaired playground for years to come.

And then, from the doors at the rear of the gym, a woman called out, "Two thousand dollars!"

A collective gasp rippled through the assembly, and everyone turned to see who'd crashed in at the last minute with such an insane offer. Several of the women were glaring daggers at the new arrival, and judging by the silence, none of them had the wherewithal to drive the price on Josh's dance up any higher.

"I can't believe it," Erin muttered, glowering at the latecomer. "What on earth is *she* doing here?"

"What's wrong?" Heather asked. "Who is that?"

"Cindy," she hissed.

The name meant nothing to Heather, but as

she rolled it around in her head, it became familiar. Eyeing the woman in the elegant black suit and stilettos, she asked, "You mean the girl who turned down Josh's proposal and left town after high school?"

"The same. I have no clue what Banker Barbie is thinking, coming here dressed like that. Or at all, for that matter."

She moved to leave, and Heather caught her arm. "Where are you going?"

"To find out what's going on. Mom will know, and if she doesn't, in about five minutes she'll have all the details."

"What about the auction?" Heather was appalled at the thought of Josh being forced to spend even a few minutes with the girl who'd once so callously broken his heart.

"I'm not thrilled with this little stunt of hers, but if Cindy's check clears, there's really nothing we can do."

Heather wasn't crazy about that answer, but recognized that the bizarre situation was out of her hands. She watched helplessly as the tall, beautifully dressed woman strolled through the crowd and met Josh in front of the podium. She gave him a bright smile that spoke of a fondness that had never died, even though she'd been gone for so long. Holding her breath, Heather forced herself to look at Josh.

He was furious.

She'd never seen that stony expression on him before, and part of her was relieved to see it now. It was apparent that Cindy had ambushed him, and he wasn't any happier to see her tonight than Heather was. As willing as he'd been to help raise money for the playground, she wondered if he was regretting it now.

When his eyes met hers, she saw an unspoken apology in them. Because she felt sorry for him, she decided that the least she could do was show him some moral support. She grabbed Erin's discarded clipboard and made her way to the front of the gym in what she hoped appeared to be an official manner.

"Good evening," she introduced herself politely, offering a hand. "I'm Heather Fitzgerald, and I wanted to thank you for your very generous bid, Miss—?"

"Cindy O'Donnell," the stunning woman replied with a practiced smile. "I apologize for getting here so late, but I drove down from the airport in Cincinnati and there was a wreck on the highway outside of Louisville."

"It seems to me you were just in time," Heather managed to say in a pleasant tone.

"I hope so," Cindy said, sending Josh a hopeful look. His face remained uncharacteristically impassive, as if he hadn't yet decided how to react to seeing his high school sweetheart again. After a few seconds, Cindy seemed to take the hint and reached into her designer bag for a leather-bound checkbook. "Who do I make the check out to?"

"The Oaks Crossing Business Association. They're in charge of rebuilding the playground."

"Playground?" Cindy echoed while she wrote.

"The one in the square," Heather explained patiently. "It was damaged in a recent storm, and we're raising money to pay for the repairs. Your donation will put us over the top."

"Happy to help," Cindy said breezily, tearing off the check with a flourish before handing it to Heather. "Anything for the home folks, right?"

Although it was plainly meant to be casual, the comment sounded forced to her, and Heather wasn't sure what to make of it any more than she knew how to handle the unexpected reappearance of the woman Josh had once planned on marrying.

The thought reminded her that he hadn't made a peep since she'd come over to join them. What was going on with him? she wondered, her earlier sympathy giving way to impatience. Then again, this was an extreme situation, so it was understandable that Josh's characteristically smooth Southern gentleman manners hadn't kicked in yet. Right?

After all he'd done for her, she owed him the benefit of the doubt. Seeking to give him some more time to get himself together, she said, "I understand you've been gone for a few years. How does it feel to be back?"

"Wonderful. I hope," she added, pinning Josh with a pleading look.

This time, a hint of a smile tugged at his mouth, and he relented a bit. "We'll see what we see."

Heather had gone this route before with a man who'd run into his former girlfriend one night at a restaurant where he'd taken Heather for dinner. One thing had led to another, and when Heather realized he'd rather be with his ex than with her, she'd hailed a taxi and gone home early. Not long after, she'd seen their engagement announcement posted on the local newspaper site when she'd been hunting for a new apartment.

Once bitten, twice shy, she thought morosely. Much as it pained her to acknowledge the fact, she knew that there was no way she could compete with the woman who'd been Josh's first love. Long ago, Cindy had captured the heart of the boy he'd once been. The man he was now might like Heather well enough, but their fledgling relationship was still in the tentative stage, easily given up for something—or someone—he wanted more.

She'd let herself believe that Josh was different from her ex-boyfriends, that he was a stand-up guy who would never let her down. Apparently, she'd been fooling herself, and that hurt just as much as being cast aside for this tall blonde beauty.

Fortunately for her, the emcee got everyone's attention and pointed out that the DJ who was running the dance portion of the evening was taking requests. Several couples went over to the table to make their choices, and Heather took the opportunity to retreat from what had become an incredibly uncomfortable situation.

Early on in the bidding, she'd resigned herself to watching Josh dance with someone other than her tonight. Never in her wildest dreams had she considered the possibility that she'd lose out to the one woman he'd ever loved enough to propose marriage to.

"Well, I've got things to wrap up behind the scenes, so I'll leave you to your reunion," she said briskly, turning away before she lost her head and made a complete fool of herself.

Her heart protested immediately, causing a

twisting sensation in her chest that made her wince. She'd been disappointed many times in her life, and some of those losses hurt worse than others. But never had she been so close to everything she wanted, only to have it snatched away from her at the last moment.

Maybe Josh felt the same way, she mused, slowing her pace to let him catch up if he wanted to talk to her. When he didn't appear by her side, she chanced a look back at the dance floor.

Josh stood apart from Cindy, arms crossed while he listened to whatever she was saying. Her anxious expression told Heather that their conversation was mostly one-way, and she was human enough to be happy about that. In her mind, the best possible outcome was for Josh to honor his obligation for one dance and then leave. Without Cindy. After all, it wasn't like she was planning to relocate to Oaks Crossing. Once she was gone, Heather would have a long talk with the good-natured farmer and learn, once and for all, what kind of future he had in mind for them.

Heather was just starting to feel more positive about things when she noticed Erin plowing through the milling crowd like a woman on a mission. The grim expression she was wearing swept away Heather's optimism as if it were nothing but smoke.

"I got the news," Erin began without preamble, "but you're not gonna like it."

"Please," Heather replied, forcing a laugh. "How bad can it be?"

"Cindy's grandparents' house is still in the family, but no one's lived in it for years. She's here to see what kind of work it needs before she can move in."

Heather's heart plummeted to the floor. "You mean, she's planning to stay here permanently?"

"That's what Mom heard." Resting a hand on Heather's shoulder, she lowered her voice. "But that doesn't mean she and Josh will get back together. Cindy's been gone for years, and it took him a long time to get over her. My little brother's a moron sometimes, but he's not stupid enough to let her hurt him again."

Erin's confidence had a hollow ring to it, and while Heather appreciated the gesture, she had to be practical. While he'd looked irritated at seeing his old girlfriend, Josh hadn't made any effort at all to explain his relationship with Heather to Cindy. Anyone with a brain would assume that meant he wasn't sure about his feelings for either one of them.

Unfortunately, tonight's strange events had

shown her exactly how she felt about him. Josh had come to mean the world to her, and she wasn't sure how to go about falling out of love with him.

Man, did he wish he'd stuck to his guns about the not-dancing thing.

If he had, Josh figured that right about now, he'd have finished his work for the day and would be spending his evening with Heather and Bailey. Instead, he was on his third dance with Cindy because she'd begged him for more time so they could talk, and he didn't know how to tell her no.

That had always been his biggest problem when it came to her, he lamented silently. When she turned those beautiful green eyes on him, he was just about helpless. Even when what she was asking him for went against his better judgment.

"So my cousin told me about the benefit tonight, and I thought it would be the perfect opening for me to tell you I've seen the light and I'm moving home," she finally wrapped up her story with a hesitant smile. "You were right all along. The big, bad world is no place for a sweet country girl like me."

The night she'd turned down his proposal, he'd told her that, hoping to convince her to stay in Oaks Crossing and share the life he'd always envisioned himself living. The trouble was, for him that dream had died years ago, and he wasn't remotely interested in reviving it. Not with her, anyway.

His lack of a response seemed to make her nervous, and she let out a shaky laugh. "Most people like to hear that they were right."

"It was a long time ago, Cindy," he hedged, searching for a way to be honest without hurting her over something that was so far in the past it barely affected him anymore. "It doesn't matter who said what."

"I found out the truth, though. And I did it the hardest way possible, believe me. Doesn't that count for something?"

Not to him, he thought, although he grudgingly gave her credit for playing the drama card to entice him into asking her for details. While it wasn't in him to be cold and uncaring, the last thing he wanted was to be subjected to the sordid details of whatever disaster had sent her back to Kentucky with her tail tucked.

Wrestling with so many conflicting emotions wasn't easy for him, but he was trying desperately to keep a rein on his temper and avoid making a scene that wouldn't solve anything and would embarrass them both. "A lot has changed since then."

"Like what?"

He growled in frustration. So much for being nice. "You really wanna do this here? Now?"

"Yes, I do," she insisted, tilting her chin in a defiant gesture that made him think of Heather. Then, in a blink, Cindy's features softened, and she gave him those doe eyes again. "Please, Josh. Five minutes, that's all I'm asking."

He certainly wasn't going to have it out with her in the middle of the gym where so many folks were watching them, probably expecting some kind of blow-up. Stepping away, he motioned for her to go ahead of him and followed her into the deserted hallway. And there, in front of the case holding the football trophies that he and his brothers had helped earn, he waited for her to continue the discussion that, to his mind, had already gone on way too long.

"So," she began in a more or less reasonable tone, "you were going to tell me how much things have changed since we last saw each other."

In answer, he looked her up and down, then allowed his disapproval of her outfit to show in his expression. "Kinda fancy for someone who claims she wants to go back to being a country girl, don't ya think?"

"These are just clothes," she informed him angrily. "I'm still the same person I always was."

That did it for him, and suddenly he didn't care who heard them. Scowling for all he was worth, he folded his arms in a gesture that made it clear he was done tiptoeing around her feelings. "Yeah? You came strutting in here like the queen of England, to make sure I noticed. To make sure *everyone* noticed. That was never your style before."

"I told you, I was late because there was an accident—"

"I don't care," he interrupted curtly. "The Cindy I used to know would never humiliate me in front of the whole town this way. She would've come by my house later so we could hash things out in private. And she never would've paid a small fortune to dance with me, just to show up everyone else."

"I didn't mean it that way," she confided in a miserable whisper. "I wanted to be sure I won so we could talk."

Her chin started trembling, and beneath the expertly applied makeup, her face contorted in what his instincts told him was genuine sorrow. When her eyes glistened with tears, he managed to hold his ground, but it was a near thing. She was a lot better at playing on his sympathy than he was at withholding it.

Summoning Mike's trademark growl, very quietly he said, "That won't work on me anymore. You made your choice about me the night I proposed, and I learned to live with it. You came home, expecting to find me right where you left me. But I'm not the same guy anymore, and no amount of waterworks is gonna change that."

With that, he turned away from her for what he prayed would be the last time. On his way out of the building, he passed several groups of people standing in line at the refreshment tables. Josh was aware of the rumble of comments he left in his wake, but he couldn't have possibly cared less.

Only one person's opinion of him mattered right now: Heather's. But in his attempt to keep things under control until he could quietly set Cindy straight, he feared that he'd blown whatever chance he might have had of winning the veterinarian's closely guarded heart. He realized now, too late, that he should have delivered his blunt parting speech while Heather was still there, so she'd know without question how serious he was about the relationship that had been gradually building between them.

Judging by her quick exit, he knew that there was no fixing the situation tonight, even if he could somehow figure out how to explain the temporary lapse in his sanity. She was angry with him for the clumsy way he'd behaved, and she had every right to be. Raised by an Irish mother whose temper could raise the roof, Josh had a healthy respect for a woman's fury and understood all too well that it was best to keep your head down until she cooled off. And hope she eventually forgave you for being an idiot.

For now, since he had no idea what else to do, he headed home. After the way his night had gone, some peace and quiet sounded good to him.

Chapter Ten

Monday morning, Heather was struggling to finish the French braid Bailey had requested in honor of the day care's return to its own building. The job wasn't easy with her model practically bouncing off the tall stool she was perched on.

"Hold still, bean," she chided, trying to keep hold of the strands that were on their way out of her grasp. "Otherwise, you'll be stuck wearing a plain old ponytail."

Immediately, the girl stopped dancing, amending the movement to a more sedate bop. "Sorry, Aunt Heather. I'm just excited. It's a big day."

"I know, and I'm thrilled you and your classmates will finally be back in your own place. Since the old decorations were ruined, Miss

Tammy told me they're going to let you guys choose how to do them over. Won't that be fun?"

"Cara's mom told us about that, so Cara and I have a million ideas already. Mrs. Simon said we're very creative."

"That was nice of her, especially since it's true." Heather bound the braid with an elastic band and quickly tied on a fresh blue ribbon that matched Bailey's sparkling eyes. Sitting back, she looked her beautiful niece over and smiled. "Very pretty. Are you ready to go?"

Bailey nodded, jumping down from her seat to put on the backpack that had been sitting fully stocked in the living room since last night. Not wanting to spoil her fun, Heather didn't bother reminding her that her lunch was still on the counter. Instead, she unzipped the pocket to add it in, then rezipped the bag and held out a hand. "Then let's go."

Partway up the street, they joined up with the Simons and headed across the square as a group. They spent the short walk chatting and laughing, and Heather was struck by how quickly she and Bailey had been accepted by the friendly residents of this small town. That thought led to another, less appealing one, and she fought to keep a smile plastered on her face.

She hadn't heard from Josh all weekend, and

two emergency surgeries at the clinic had kept her from attending church on Sunday. Thanks to Cindy O'Donnell's unexpected appearance, the dance had ended on a cliff-hanger worthy of a hit TV series, and Heather wasn't sure where things stood with Josh. He'd promised Bailey that he'd be here this morning for the grand reopening, and under normal circumstances, it wouldn't have occurred to her to question the commitment he'd made.

But these weren't normal circumstances, and she casually glanced over at the cars parked in the lot, looking for his pickup. When she saw it there, she chided herself for being silly. She should have known that, no matter what had gone on between them, he'd never let Bailey down. It simply wasn't in him to disappoint a child.

Still, she feared that this wasn't likely to go well, and as they went through the house's antique glass-front door, she braced herself for some uncomfortable moments until the party was over. When they stepped into the bright, airy lobby, Bailey deserted her to greet friends who were obviously as elated to be back as she was. Heather stood near the door, taking in the repairs and outright improvements that had been made to the stately old building.

So many windows had been broken in the

storm that the contractor had replaced them all, and the light streaming through them gave the interior a sunny appearance that welcomed children and parents alike. Soft colors on the walls were the perfect backdrop to the kids' artwork, paintings and drawings showing everything from rolling fields to lush forests to family portraits. As Heather strolled along the walls admiring them, one in particular caught her eye, and she paused for a closer look.

"My family, by Bailey Fitzgerald."

Below the slightly crooked title was a little girl holding a kitten, obviously Bailey and Annabelle. Beside them stood a taller version of the girl, and overhead were winged figures of a light-haired woman and a man in a blue baseball cap, watching over everything. Everyone looked happy, which suggested to Heather that her niece had finally come to terms with the loss of her parents.

"I'm no art expert, but that's a real pretty picture."

Josh's mellow drawl came from behind her, and Heather waited a beat to collect herself before turning to face him. After what had gone on at the dance, she had no doubt that people were watching them closely, so she kept her tone light to avoid attracting any more attention than necessary. "Thanks. I'll tell her you said so."

"Already did." Leaning in, he added, "I always check out the snacks first thing. If you get there too late, all they've got left is warm juice and wheat crackers."

She laughed, which was clearly what he wanted, but he was acting as if nothing had happened Friday night. Instead he was smiling and cracking jokes, being his usual charming self. The problem was, she was still smarting over the way he'd neglected to introduce her to Cindy and explain that Heather was the new woman in his life. Maybe she'd misread his attention all along, she thought morosely. Maybe he'd decided that he was satisfied with them being friends and wasn't interested in anything more.

Unfortunately, she wouldn't know for sure unless she asked him straight out how he viewed their relationship. But she'd never done that with a man in her life, and she wasn't about to stoop that low now. If he wanted to pursue a romantic future with her, fine. If not, fine. It really didn't matter to her one way or the other.

Before that defiant thought was even finished, though, another, gentler one drifted in to remind her that Josh's unspoken plans for them did in fact matter to her. Very much.

"Sierra mentioned yesterday that we're getting low on straw bedding for the baby barn," Heather commented, giving him an opening to make arrangements to stop by the clinic for a reason other than speaking to her.

"I'm swamped right now, but tell her I'll bring some down later in the week."

Heather waited for him to say something else, give her one of those heart-stopping grins, anything that would tell her he'd gotten the hint.

But he didn't.

Fighting off her disappointment, she decided that she'd been too subtle and tried one more time. "The otters are nearly ready to go, if you want to come by and see them before we release them."

"That'd be cool. Thanks for letting me know."

"You're welcome." Josh had always been so up-front with her that she knew that his cluelessness wasn't an act. He really had no idea she was still upset. Or maybe he'd never known it in the first place. Out of pride, she did her best to hide the fact that she was terribly disappointed to discover that she'd misunderstood his intentions toward her. And that, contrary to her earlier belief, he really was like every other man she'd known.

Thankfully, Bailey left her circle of friends and skipped over to join them near the art wall. "Do you like my painting, Aunt Heather?"

"It's beautiful." Heather drew her in for a hug that felt comforting to herself, too. She didn't need a man to make her life feel rewarding when she had Bailey around. "I'm sure your parents are thrilled that you drew them so well."

"I don't remember Mommy, so I drew her to look like the picture on my night table. I made sure Daddy was wearing his favorite hat. I couldn't do a little *D* for the Tigers, but I think he'd like it."

Heather's throat clogged with remorse for all the wonderful things Craig was missing with his daughter, and she swallowed hard before speaking. "He'd love it, bean. He was always so proud of you."

"I still miss him," Bailey said, looking at the picture somberly, then up at Heather. "But I'm glad I have you."

"And I'm glad I have you," Heather murmured as tears welled in her eyes. Reaching out, she flipped Bailey's wandering braid over her shoulder and then gave her a gentle shove.

"You'd better go get some of those ginger snaps before they're all gone."

"Okay. Do you want some, too?"

"No, thank you."

Unfazed, Bailey trained her clear blue eyes on their guest. "How about you, Josh? You like cookies."

"I sure do. Lead the way."

He held out his hand, and she took it without hesitation, chattering like a delighted blue jay while she led him over to the treats. Heather watched them go, her heart sinking a little with each step they took together. As fond as she'd been of Josh, she worried that Bailey had become far too attached to the tall country boy who seemed to have dismissed the idea of anything beyond friendship with Heather.

Heather could live with that, because she had to. But she had no idea how she was going to explain it to Bailey.

"Are you sure?" Erin asked, frowning in obvious disappointment. "Friday night you seemed really excited about staying here long term."

She had been, Heather admitted glumly. What a difference a few days made. Since her boss knew perfectly well what had happened, she saw no reason to be coy. "Things have changed since then."

"I'm not sure you know this, but Cindy's not coming back here, after all. Cam heard that she snuck out of town early Saturday morning. Stood up the contractor she'd arranged to meet without even paying his consultation fee."

"I heard. Several times." Heather understood that people meant well, but having her personal life grinding around in the gossip mill didn't exactly thrill her. In a bustling city, that kind of nonsense would never happen, because no one would care about what was going on with her, romantic or otherwise. Mostly because no one would know who she was. Regaining the anonymity she'd once enjoyed alternately appealed to her and dismayed her, until she felt lost in an endless loop of confusion.

"I wouldn't dream of telling you what to do, but I hope you'll take a couple more days to think it over. I'd hate for you to make a decision while you're upset that you and Bailey might regret later."

Mention of her niece made Heather's stomach churn, and she felt a whine threatening to burst free of her control. She'd spent the entire weekend turning the options over in her mind, this way and that, until she was so tied up in knots, she couldn't think straight anymore.

One minute, she was convinced that she could still make things work in Oaks Crossing. She and Bailey had been so happy here, she hated to uproot them both again to start over somewhere else. The next, she remembered that Josh was not only her boss's brother, but he was a constant presence in the fields surrounding the rescue center, not to mention in town. Could she really forget about what had almost happened between them? Or would she think of those sweet stolen moments every time she saw him and be sad all over again?

Apparently, her silence inspired Erin, because she reached out to rub Heather's shoulder in a comforting gesture. "When do you have to give that Louisville clinic their answer?"

"They know I have Bailey and her school to consider, so they gave me a week to decide."

"That's good."

Was it? Or was it better to make a clean break and move on? After all, Cindy had done it, and evidently was very successful now. The same approach could work for Heather, too. Unfortunately, as soon as the thought flitted through her mind, she recognized it for the false bravado that it was.

Surgical, clean breaks had been her style once, but not anymore. Her practical, uncomplicated life was now anything but, and there was more to the equation than there used to be. Out of necessity, the driven woman she'd been for so long had given way to someone who'd learned how to stop and listen to what her heart was telling her.

Bailey had begun teaching her how to do that, and Josh had deftly picked up the lesson, driving it home in a gentle, no-pressure way that only he could have managed. The idea of losing out on something so precious made her unspeakably sad, but she'd never been one to beg for a man's attention, and she wasn't about to start now. If he didn't want her, she wouldn't degrade herself by trying to convince him otherwise.

"Well, I'll get out of your hair," Erin said on her way to the lobby door. Turning back, she gave Heather a sympathetic smile. "If you decide you'd like someone to talk to, I'm a good listener who doesn't repeat what she hears."

"I'll remember that. Thanks."

With a quick wave, Erin left Heather alone in the cheerful reception area. Posters of adopted animals decorated the walls, chronicling the clinic's success in placing abandoned pets with loving families. There were also photos of wild animals that ran the gamut from Teddy, the orphaned bear cub, to the family of otters they'd be releasing soon. Her favorite was a shot of Drew and Bekah near the woods behind the center, standing together hand in hand as they watched a beautiful red-tailed hawk circling in a clear autumn sky.

It reminded her of her first day at work, when Josh had dropped what he was doing to help them tend to Annabelle and her siblings. That morning, she'd had no clue just how important he would eventually become to both her and Bailey.

Then again, if he hadn't proved to be so wonderful, the choice to take the higher-paying job she'd been offered in Louisville would be a no-brainer. Which left her back where she'd started.

Should she stay or should she go? It was the most straightforward decision anyone could make. She'd made many of them herself and had always been content with the results. She'd simply examined the alternatives and picked the best one for her—and later for Bailey. Easy.

This time, her heart wanted one thing while her brain was arguing for the opposite. In the past, she'd have followed the most logical path without reservation, confident that it would lead her to where she needed to be. But this time, she wasn't so sure. The choices weren't as clear-cut, and even her reliable pro-con lists had proved to be no help at all.

Hoping that might have changed, she pulled the folded-up sheet of paper from the pocket of her lab coat and smoothed it out on the counter. On one side was a long list of reasons to go, including more money, health care benefits and the excitement that came from living in a vibrant city. On the other was just one item: home. The single word looked lonely in its column, but the meaning of it resonated deeply.

Here in Oaks Crossing, she and Bailey had begun stitching together a life that included more new friends than she could have anticipated making. Not to mention Annabelle, who somehow became fluffier and more adorable every day. The kitten would come with them, of course, but what about the Kinleys and Bailey's school friends, and everyone else?

What about Josh? Whatever was going on between the two of them, he'd kept his word to Bailey, and Heather couldn't help admiring him for that. Erin seemed confident that Cindy had left town for good, which was positive news.

So why hadn't he called her? Heather wondered for the hundredth time. She supposed he might be waiting for her to contact him, but she wasn't the one who'd ignored him because an old flame showed up and rattled her cage. In her mind, it was up to him to make the effort to reconnect with her, difficult as that first step might be for him.

Her temper began simmering again, and she had to acknowledge that as rational as her argument sounded in her head, the upshot was that she was still mad about the whole messy situation. She was glad to know that Cindy was no longer in the picture, but that still left the issue of why Josh hadn't spoken up at the dance about being involved with Heather. Quite honestly, the whole thing gave her a headache.

As the phone began to ring, she put aside her dilemma and focused on work, grateful for a distraction from the thorniest problem she'd ever had to solve.

Thursday morning, Josh stood back from the climbing rope he'd just finished installing at the playground, eyeballing the height of the large knot at the bottom from the ground to make sure kids could reach it easily. Satisfied with his handiwork, he stood at the base of it and looked up at the landing that branched off in both directions to either the original castle or the tower they'd be adding during the final phase of the reconstruction.

His tower, Erin had crowed proudly when she informed him that Cindy's check for a dance with him had cleared and allowed the committee to purchase the materials for the addition. Abby and Parker were psyched about the change, and Cam's design for the new section was almost done. The plan was to have it ready by the end of June, and Josh smiled when he imagined kids crawling all over it, laughing and yelling while they enjoyed a fresh challenge.

The voices weren't only in his mind, he realized, turning to see that he was no longer alone at the playground. Running toward him, calling his name, was Bailey. Today her hair was in a ponytail, secured with a pink ribbon that was unraveling as she raced over and nearly bowled him over with an exuberant hug.

Tilting her head back, she grinned up at him. "Hi."

"Hi yourself, sweetness," he said, reaching out to retie and double-knot the ribbon. "What's shakin'?"

"I won the art contest at school today," she told him excitedly. "I entered a picture I drew of Gideon, the big *beggin* horse at the farm."

"Belgian," he corrected her with a chuckle. "And congratulations."

"Thank you." Her smiled dimmed a bit, and

she asked, "Where have you been? I haven't seen you in forever."

"Just busy is all," he hedged, unwilling to lie but wary of upsetting her.

"So is Aunt Heather. There are lots of new animals at the shelter that need her help."

Josh wasn't keen on discussing Heather with anyone, so he changed the subject. "How's that cutie Annabelle doing?"

"Good. She can climb the curtains in our living room all the way to the top now, so we put the sofa under the window in case she falls."

"Good thinking." Josh noticed one of the teachers headed their way, and he held up a hand in acknowledgment. "Looks like you should get going. I'll see you soon."

"When?"

Good question, he thought glumly. He'd messed up with Heather big-time, and while he wasn't usually shy about admitting a mistake and taking his medicine, this was different. He knew he'd let her down, and he had no idea how to make it up to her. Unfortunately, that left him with dodging the Fitzgerald girls altogether, which obviously hadn't worked out too well. He should've stayed at the farm.

"When I can."

She took a step away from him, then turned

back and gave him the most wistful look he'd ever seen. "Did I do something to make you mad?"

"Never." Josh's heart seized up knowing that this bright, sweet child could even think something like that. Hunkering down to her level, he wrapped her in an embrace and then held her at arm's length. "You're sweet and smart, and you never cause anyone a bit of trouble. I think you might be the best kid ever. Just don't tell Abby and Parker I said so."

"Okaaaaaay." By the way she dragged out her reply, he could tell she didn't quite believe him, but she didn't press. "Thank you for putting up the rope. I really like climbing."

Then she gave him a quick hug and joined the teacher waiting for her at the edge of the play area. As they walked back to where the other day care kids were playing kickball, Bailey cast several glances over her shoulder at him. The sadness on her face nearly did him in, and Josh had to force his boots to stay rooted where they belonged instead of trailing after her like a love-starved hound.

That's what you get, he complained to himself as he packed up his tools and walked over to his truck. *You had to go and fall in love with both of them, and now you're a lost cause.*

Frustrated beyond measure, he threw his toolbox on the floor, then climbed into the cab and slammed the door shut before pulling onto Main Street. He followed it out of town, not really headed anywhere in particular. Fresh air flowed through the open windows, and he felt it blowing away some of his sour mood.

As he came around a curve, he noticed something lying prone on the side of the road and pulled up behind it to investigate. Approaching slowly, he saw it was a mixed-breed dog that had been hit by a car. The poor thing was still breathing, but its attempts to move were weak, at best. It wore no collar, but the faint thumping of its tail told Josh that it recognized him as someone who might be there to offer him some help.

"Hey there, boy," Josh murmured, slowly moving closer. "Not such a good day for you, huh?"

The dog whimpered faintly, brown eyes imploring him to quit yakking and do something constructive. Careful to disturb him as little as possible, Josh swept up the bleeding dog and rested him on the passenger side of the pickup's bench seat. The nearest animal clinic was the rescue center, and while he wasn't keen on having an encounter with Heather just now, there was no way he'd let this poor animal suffer when she was so close by.

He drove as quickly as he dared, checking on his passenger frequently. "Hang in there, buddy. Almost there."

The tail thumped again, as if the mutt understood what Josh was saying to him. When they arrived at the center, he wasted no time getting the injured dog inside. To her credit, Heather never even blinked at him. Efficient as always, she came around the front counter and did a quick inspection of the dog in his arms. "Not awful, but not great, either. Bring him on back, and we'll get a better idea what we're dealing with."

Hello to you, too, Josh thought wryly as he followed her through the door into an exam room. As he gently set the dog on the metal table, he said, "I found him a couple of miles from here. No collar, but he seems pretty tame to me."

"You mean, because he didn't bite you?" she asked without looking up from her examination.

"Well, yeah."

"Dogs are pretty smart. He probably knew you wanted to help, so he didn't hurt you. Besides that, he's lost some blood, and he's got a bump on his temple. He's not in any shape to do much damage to anyone."

"He'll be okay, though, right?" When she glanced up at Josh, he winced at the shuttered look in the eyes that had once looked on him with such fondness. "I mean, you can fix him up?"

"I hope so."

Josh got the distinct impression that she was pulling the professional sympathy routine on him, and he bristled at the cool treatment. "Heather, this is me. You can give it to me straight."

"What I need is an X-ray, but we don't have the equipment for that. So I have to do this the old-fashioned way, poking and prodding. It'll hurt him, and he's not going to like it, but I don't have a choice."

The idea of walking away and leaving her with a squirming, potentially dangerous animal didn't sit right with him. "I can stay and hold him for you. If you want," he added quickly, wary of insulting the feisty vet by suggesting that he doubted she could manage on her own.

After a moment, she nodded. "That would be helpful, for both him and me. If you're sure you have the time."

The overly polite tone grated on his nerves, but Josh forced a smile. "No problem."

Following her instructions, he got a firm hold on her patient and closed his eyes, sending up a quick prayer for the injured dog. When he realized that she wasn't doing anything, he glanced up at her and found her studying him intently.

"Are you praying for this dog?"

"Well, yeah." Fearing that she might take that as him questioning her skill, he explained, "Just asking for a little extra help is all."

The clinical expression gave way to a much softer one, and she slowly shook her head. "You really are the sweetest guy on the planet, aren't you?"

Sensing that her icy opinion of him was starting to thaw, he grinned. "I try."

She gave him a long, thoughtful look but didn't say anything else before turning her attention back to her work. After confirming which bones were broken and which were intact, she gave the dog a couple of injections. Then she carefully cleaned and wrapped his wounds, ending her treatment with a gentle scratch between his ears.

She explained each step to the animal, speaking to him in a calm, comforting tone that reminded Josh of Doc Sheppard. Confident and reassuring, it was the kind of manner that he suspected less empathetic people couldn't even hope to mimic. You either had it or you didn't.

When she was finished, Josh carried their new guest into the kennel and settled him on a pad in a large crate that gave him enough room to stretch out. The scruffy guy laid his head down and let out a relieved canine sigh. Knowing that the situation could have ended much differently, Josh left the kennel feeling pretty good about himself.

Until it occurred to him that Heather was gone.

No goodbye, no thank-you, nothing. Being a Kinley boy, Josh had never chased after a woman in his life. Ordinarily, he would've taken her quick departure to mean she wasn't interested in him anymore.

Then again, he thought as he strolled down the hallway that led to her office, this was far from an ordinary situation for him. If Heather had decided that she didn't want anything more to do with him, he could live with that. But he wasn't going to slink around town, hoping he wouldn't run into her or her niece somewhere. His encounter with Bailey earlier had proved to him that his feelings for both of them ran deep and hadn't faded any in the past few days.

If anything, seeing Heather again had made him more determined to have it out with her so they could figure out where they stood, one way or the other. He was a pretty straightforward guy, and not knowing the truth was driving him crazy.

But he drew the line at stalking. So rather than barge into her office, he waited until she'd hung her jacket on the rack behind her desk, and then he politely knocked on the metal jamb.

When she angled her head toward him, the unreadable look on her face clearly said that she knew who was knocking. "Yes?"

The stiff response knocked him off his stride for a second, but he reminded himself that he was on a mission to settle things between them. Strolling in, he opened with a compliment. "You did a great job with that old mutt."

"Thank you."

He waited for her to go on, but she didn't. They stood there separated by her desk, staring at each other like two old-time gunfighters biding their time until the other one either drew or walked away. After a lot of brain-racking, he'd come to recognize that he was the one who'd messed up, so Josh took a deep breath and let his heart do the talking.

"I'm sorry."

* * *

Heather's jaw fell open in astonishment.

She'd been fully expecting him to remind her that he didn't know Cindy would be visiting, much less bidding on his dance. Or offer an excuse about how he'd volunteered for the fund-raiser to benefit the kids and had no control over which bidder he ended up dancing with. Or any number of lame explanations that would have been perfectly logical but would still end up making her angrier than ever.

Instead, he'd apologized. Simply, and without prodding from her, without asking what he'd done wrong. Instinct told her that he wasn't totally onboard with why she was so upset with him, but that he understood it was somehow his fault. And, because he cared about her, he was sorry for what he'd done. The stunning honesty of it was almost more than she could process, and she did what she usually did in a situation when she didn't know how to react.

She took a step back and asked for clarification. "For what?"

"For being a moron. Cindy blindsided me, showing up like that, and I didn't handle it right."

His heartfelt confession broke through her lingering anger, and the courage he'd shown made her more generous than she might have been if he'd rattled off a long list of excuses. "I didn't, either. Guys haven't always treated me very well, so I'm sensitive about that kind of thing. At the dance, it felt like you wanted to be with her instead of me, and I thought that was why you didn't tell her about us."

"Not a chance. Cindy and I were done a long time ago, and she's got no place in my life now. I told her that Friday night." In his eyes blazed an intensity she hadn't seen there before, and he went on. "I don't know what's gonna happen with us now, but no matter what, I wanted you to know that you mean a lot to me. So does Bailey, and I'd never intentionally do anything to hurt either of you."

"I know," she said without thinking. Then, because things were even more of a mess than he realized, she sighed. "You'll find out sooner or later, so I should tell you now. I accepted the job offer from that animal hospital in Louisville."

"Why?"

The dejection in that single word knifed through her heart, and she felt as if she'd just kicked a loyal hound for being in her way. "The usual reasons—large clinic, large salary, great schools for Bailey. We can have a nice house, and I can pay off my loans before they drown me. In six years, I'll be a full-fledged partner in the business, and that will give us the security I want."

Refusing to honor the barrier she'd intentionally placed between them, Josh circled around her desk and stepped directly into her personal space. "What about us?"

"What about us?" she echoed tartly, glaring up at him. "Friday night, it was like I didn't even exist."

Again, she waited for the excuses. And again, he surprised her. Hanging his head like a shamed little boy, he heaved a sigh before meeting her eyes. "I know. I'm not good with drama."

It struck her as being an odd thing to say, and she frowned. "What does that mean?"

"I'm from an Irish family, and we lay everything out on the table, whether someone's gonna like it or not. Being ambushed like that really threw me, and I didn't know what to do, so I froze. I know it sounds stupid, but it's the truth."

And hard to argue with, she thought. "Okay, I get that. But why are you telling me this now? Didn't you hear me say I'm leaving for Louisville soon?"

"Things can change," he reminded her gently, taking another step toward her. He didn't touch her, but the emotion blazing in his eyes warmed her from head to toe. "You can change 'em if you want to."

Did she want to? she wondered. Part of her did, the hopeful girl who still lived inside her and had found a place in the light when Josh's playful nature had gradually encouraged her to come out and enjoy herself. But the other part, the responsible adult who had a lot of obligations to meet, hesitated.

As if he sensed her confusion, he slid his arms around her and drew her close enough to catch the fresh scent of soap and hay on his T-shirt. "Y'know, I just remembered something."

"What's that?"

"I still owe you a dance."

The mischief twinkling in his eyes was infectious, and she couldn't resist playing along. "Yes, you do."

"I'd never go back on my word to a lady. Hang on a sec." Picking her phone up off her desk, he cued up something from her playlist.

When the song they'd first waltzed to came from the small speakers, she laughed. "There's not a lot of room in here."

"Then we'll have to get cozy," he replied, reeling her in for a gesture that was half smile and half kiss. "You don't mind, do you?"

"Not a bit." Breaking all the rules of proper ballroom etiquette, she snuggled against him with a blissful sigh. "I love you, Josh."

"Love you, too," he replied, dropping a kiss on the top of her head. "And I promise that if you'll take a shot with me, I'll do everything I can to make sure you never regret it. Would that work for you?"

"Yes," she murmured against his chest. "That works for me."

Epilogue

Heather soon discovered that autumn at Gallimore Stables was even more hectic than the rest of the seasons.

Of course, this year the Kinley clan had welcomed two new cousins into the mix. Drew and Bekah's son, Caleb, had arrived a week early but perfect, and a few weeks later, Erin's request for another girl at the farm had been granted. Seated around the large table that always seemed to have plenty of space for everyone who came by for Sunday lunches, Lily was rocking Grace, staring down at her with pure love shining in her eyes.

"She's such a good baby," big sister Abby informed them proudly. "She only fusses when she's hungry."

"Yeah, don't we all?" Josh commented from

his place on the opposite bench. "Everything smells great, Mom. Can't we start now?"

"No, you can't," she scolded, smacking his hand as he reached out to snag a roll from a towel-covered basket. "I'm still pulling things out of the oven, which you can see perfectly well."

"Okay." But when she turned her back, he sneaked a biscuit and broke off a piece for each of the dogs before popping the flaky evidence in his mouth.

"I saw that," Heather warned in a hushed voice.

"I know you can keep a secret, though."

"Another one?" she complained in a fake whine. "How many is that now?"

"I dunno. I'm not really a numbers guy." Grinning, he kissed her cheek as he slid over to make room for Bailey. "Let's just say I'll pay my debt in a couple of weeks at the Oaks Crossing Harvest Dance."

"I'm going to hold you to that."

Her stern tone made him laugh. "You don't have to threaten me, sweetheart. I offered."

"That's so nice," Bailey chimed in, pigtails bobbing as she looked from one of them to the other. "You call Aunt Heather sweetheart and me sweetness. They kind of go together."

"They sure do," he agreed, giving her a

fond smile. The one he trained on Heather had a more romantic vibe to it, and she felt her cheeks beginning to warm.

Fortunately, she was distracted by an unfamiliar car pulling into the turnaround out front. After glancing around the kitchen and seeing the entire crew, she looked out the window in confusion. "Did your mom invite someone else today? I thought everyone was already here."

"Almost everyone," Josh replied in a cryptic tone that was totally unlike him.

Standing, he went to the door and strolled out toward the driveway. When she saw whom he was going to meet, Heather bolted after him like a shot.

"Mom! Dad!" she called out, overjoyed to see them so unexpectedly. She gave them each a hug and then added, "What a wonderful surprise! I thought you weren't coming back from Italy until just before the holidays."

"Well, we decided we couldn't stay away that long," her father said, trading a look with Josh before they shook hands. "It's a pleasure to finally meet you, son. We've heard a lot of good things about you."

"Same here, sir. Mrs. Fitzgerald."

He flashed her one of those infernal grins,

and she laughed. "I see what my daughter meant about you being a shameless charmer."

"No shame in being friendly," he assured her smoothly. "You've had a long trip from the airport, so you must be parched. Come on inside and meet the rest of us."

Heather had learned early on that extra guests didn't faze the Kinleys at all, and places were quickly set for her parents. Maggie got the conversation started easily enough. She sat down beside them and asked about their tour of Ireland. They put their heads together over their phones to flip through pictures from their adventures, and it turned out that they'd been exploring the same area where Maggie's family originally emigrated from when she was a baby.

"Small world," Josh murmured to Heather as he passed along a platter of roast beef so tender, it barely held together on the serving fork.

"Smaller all the time," she agreed. "Isn't it great how well they're getting along? It's like they've known each other for years."

"We Irish are a friendly people. It's genetic."

She gave him a wry smile. "Some of us more than others."

"What? You liked me well enough when we met."

"Have you ever met a woman who didn't?"

He looked up at the beamed ceiling as if searching for an answer. When he came back to her with a slow grin, she rolled her eyes. "I'll take that as a no."

"Good plan."

Since she'd made the decision to put roots down in this lovely little town, her relationship with Josh had blossomed into more than she'd ever dared to hope for. Their amusing bouts of sparring had become high points of days that were fulfilling but could be long and emotional at times. Bailey was happily attending the Oaks Crossing preschool, and Cara had shown herself to be the kind of fun and loyal best friend every girl needed.

In the end, the path that Heather had chosen out of desperation had proved to be the right one for them. And, while she was proud of the difficult choices she'd made, she now recognized that those decisions hadn't been hers alone.

God had led her here, to a place where she felt valued and appreciated. On that same path, He'd placed a good-hearted country boy who had the wisdom to let her be who she was, all while standing solidly behind her in case she needed his help. That someone like Josh had come into her life at precisely the right moment was the greatest blessing she could have asked for.

While the rest of the family was lingering over their meal, Josh leaned in and murmured, "I'm stuffed, but if I don't eat dessert, Mom'll think I'm sick or something. You girls wanna take a walk with me?"

"Sure!"

Bailey hopped up and raced out the door, while Heather excused them both and followed after her at a more leisurely pace. Josh stopped only long enough to put on the jean jacket that he'd hung on the back of his chair, and joined her to go down the porch steps. Once they were outside in the yard, he draped an arm around her shoulders, not seeming to be in much of a hurry. They trailed behind Bailey, who'd made a beeline for the white fence that enclosed the front pasture.

Heather had visited here enough throughout the spring and summer to know that the scenic farm was beautiful all year long. But fall was her favorite season, and the Kentucky hills that surrounded the Kinleys' acreage were even more breathtaking dressed in their autumn colors. Leaves on the trees were turning in a blaze of red and gold, a vivid contrast to the ever-present bluegrass that had given this part of the state its nickname. Unlike Detroit, which was already getting frosty at night this time of year, the Southern climate was still warm, and she had to admit that she was looking forward to a winter that didn't involve her breaking out her arctic gear.

"So," Josh said as they strolled along, "I took in the last load of ethanol corn yesterday."

"And?"

"Well, we're not exactly rich, but it was enough to bring Mike's blood pressure down. Next year, we'll expand that crop and it'll be even better."

"That's wonderful, Josh. You took a chance, and it paid off." Thrilled by his success, she smiled up at him. "I'm sure your father is really proud of you."

"I hope so. Anyway, now that I'm back down to regular farmwork, I've got time on my hands."

His leading tone made her laugh. "Does that mean you'll be starting on my new office soon?"

"Cam finished the plans a few days ago, so how does tomorrow sound?"

"Fabulous. I've got my network of college friends hunting up used equipment for me. Sometimes larger clinics replace perfectly good things because they want the latest and greatest, and that means they have stuff collecting dust in their storerooms. I've already got a lead on an X-ray machine and some lightly used surgical lights."

"Awesome," he commented in typical Josh fashion. "At this rate, you'll be running your own practice in no time."

"It's pretty amazing," she agreed, reaching around to give him a sideways hug. "But without you, it would still just be a dream."

Smiling down at her, he dropped in for a quick kiss before they joined Bailey near the fence. When two of the ponies realized that they had company, they came over to the rail to see what was going on outside their grassy home. They sniffed at Bailey through the boards, then gave her what Heather could only describe as accusing looks.

Apparently, they were expecting to be fed, and her niece made a regretful sound. "Oh, that's too bad. We didn't bring them anything."

"Didn't we?" Josh fished some carrots from a front pocket of his jacket and offered them to her. "Now, hold your palm out flat when you're feeding them, like Mike showed you. That way, they won't nip your fingers thinking they're vegetables."

She nodded eagerly, taking the chunks from him and following his instructions. "Here you go, Sparkle and Tinkerbell."

After a cautious sniff, the animals daintily took their treats from her. As they munched, Bailey giggled. "I think they're smiling at me."

"'Course they are," Josh assured her. "Ponies appreciate getting a little extra attention just like anyone else does."

He gave Heather a nudging look, and she shook her head. "All right, you've convinced me. Bailey can start taking riding lessons with Mike on Saturdays."

"Really?" Eyes glowing joyfully, she gave Heather an exuberant hug before beaming up at Josh with a grateful expression. "I promise to work really hard in the barn with you."

"I don't doubt that for a second. But before we get to that, I need to ask you ladies something."

His normally laid-back drawl held a tinge of something she hadn't heard in it before, and Heather's mind ticked through a list of possibilities as he led them to a nearby picnic table. Once she and Bailey were seated, he stared down at them for a long, thoughtful moment.

And then he went down on one knee.

He gazed up at them with so much love in his eyes, Heather gulped back a rush of emotions that had rushed to the surface and were threatening to choke her.

"The day when I first met you two, my life

got better in more ways than I can count. Every morning, you give me reasons to get up that have nothing to do with the weather or how much work I have ahead of me."

Pausing, he reached into the other pocket of his jacket and pulled out two identical blue velvet boxes. Handing one to each of them, he went on. "I'm not great when it comes to putting the right words together, but I love you both more than I ever imagined possible. Will you ladies marry me?"

"Marry you?" Heather squeaked, opening her box to find a lovely filigree setting of gold around a sparkling diamond.

Beside her, Bailey did the same and held hers up for Heather to see. "Look, Aunt Heather! Mine is just like yours, but a little smaller."

"Well, your hand is smaller," Josh explained as he gallantly put the ring on for her.

Meeting Heather's eyes, he gave her a hesitant look that was rare for him. "What about you? Do you like yours, too?"

Heather blinked to be sure that she was seeing straight, then smiled and slowly nodded. "Yes, I do. But I like the man giving it to me even better."

Pretending to wipe nervous sweat from his forehead, he took the beautiful setting from the box and slid it into place on her finger. He punctuated the romantic gesture with a mischievous grin. "Yeah? How much better?"

In answer, she gave him a long kiss that she hoped would answer him better than any words ever could. And then, the odd sequence of events on what should have been a regular Sunday afternoon hit her, and she gasped. "You brought my parents home from Europe early, didn't you?"

"Not exactly." Chuckling, he explained. "I got their number from Erin, because she had them listed in your employee file as your next of kin. Then I called them to ask for their permission to propose to you, and they asked me to wait so they could be here, too. Longest two weeks of my life."

Now the tears welling in her eyes were more than she could blink away, and she didn't even bother trying. Framing his handsome face in her hands, she kissed him. "Joshua Kinley, you are without a doubt the sweetest, most thoughtful man ever born."

"Isn't that what you love most about me?"

"Yes," she replied with a grateful smile. "It certainly is."

* * * * *

Dear Reader,

Whether this is the first of my books that you've read or the latest of several, you've probably figured out that I love animals. Writing about a farm dedicated to rescuing them was a joy for me. Throughout the series, Erin Kinley kept searching for a permanent veterinarian to fill the open spot at the rescue center that's so important to her and the entire Kinley clan. When a friend of Josh's recommended someone, I knew this woman was destined to become part of the fabric of this charming Kentucky town.

The moment Heather Fitzgerald stepped into the spotlight, it was obvious that she was just what easygoing Josh needed: a challenge. As an added bonus, her niece Bailey adored him from the start, and before long Heather agreed with her. They brought new elements into Josh's life that he didn't even know he was missing. And Josh's deeply held faith and unwavering support of the Fitzgerald girls helped them get through a difficult time and come out the other side stronger than ever.

This is the final chapter for the Kinleys, but there are plenty more stories on the horizon. Stop by www.miaross.com for a sneak peek at what's coming. You'll also find me online on Facebook, Twitter and Goodreads. While you're there, send me a message in your favorite format. I'd love to hear from you!

Mia Ross

LARGER-PRINT BOOKS!

GET 2 FREE LARGER-PRINT NOVELS PLUS 2 FREE MYSTERY GIFTS

Love Inspired®
SUSPENSE
RIVETING INSPIRATIONAL ROMANCE

Larger-print novels are now available...

REQUEST YOUR FREE BOOKS!
2 FREE WHOLESOME ROMANCE NOVELS IN LARGER PRINT
PLUS 2
FREE
MYSTERY GIFTS

✼✼✼✼✼✼✼✼✼✼✼✼✼✼✼✼✼✼✼✼✼✼✼✼

HEARTWARMING™

✼✼✼✼✼✼✼✼✼✼✼✼✼✼✼✼✼✼✼✼✼✼✼✼

Wholesome, tender romances

YES! Please send me 2 FREE Harlequin® Heartwarming Larger-Print novels and my 2 FREE mystery gifts (gifts worth about $10). After receiving them, if I don't wish to receive any more books, I can return the shipping statement marked "cancel." If I don't cancel, I will receive 4 brand-new larger-print novels every month and be billed just $5.24 per book in the U.S. or $5.99 per book in Canada. That's a savings of at least 19% off the cover price. It's quite a bargain! Shipping and handling is just 50¢ per book in the U.S. and 75¢ per book in Canada.* I understand that accepting the 2 free books and gifts places me under no obligation to buy anything. I can always return a shipment and cancel at any time. Even if I never buy another book, the two free books and gifts are mine to keep forever.

161/361 IDN GHX2

Name	(PLEASE PRINT)
Address	Apt. #
City	State/Prov.	Zip/Postal Code

Signature (if under 18, a parent or guardian must sign)

Mail to the **Reader Service:**
IN U.S.A.: P.O. Box 1867, Buffalo, NY 14240-1867
IN CANADA: P.O. Box 609, Fort Erie, Ontario L2A 5X3

* Terms and prices subject to change without notice. Prices do not include applicable taxes. Sales tax applicable in N.Y. Canadian residents will be charged applicable taxes. Offer not valid in Quebec. This offer is limited to one order per household. Not valid for current subscribers to Harlequin Heartwarming larger-print books. All orders subject to credit approval. Credit or debit balances in a customer's account(s) may be offset by any other outstanding balance owed by or to the customer. Please allow 4 to 6 weeks for delivery. Offer available while quantities last.

Your Privacy—The Reader Service is committed to protecting your privacy. Our Privacy Policy is available online at www.ReaderService.com or upon request from the Reader Service.

We make a portion of our mailing list available to reputable third parties that offer products we believe may interest you. If you prefer that we not exchange your name with third parties, or if you wish to clarify or modify your communication preferences, please visit us at www.ReaderService.com/consumerschoice or write to us at Reader Service Preference Service, P.O. Box 9062, Buffalo, NY 14240-9062. Include your complete name and address.

HW15

WESTERN WP PROMISES

YES! Please send me **The Western Promises Collection** in Larger Print. This collection begins with 3 FREE books and 2 FREE gifts (gifts valued at approx. $14.00 retail) in the first shipment, along with the other first 4 books from the collection! If I do not cancel, I will receive 8 monthly shipments until I have the entire 51-book Western Promises collection. I will receive 2 or 3 FREE books in each shipment and I will pay just $4.99 US/ $5.89 CDN for each of the other four books in each shipment, plus $2.99 for shipping and handling per shipment. *If I decide to keep the entire collection, I'll have paid for only 32 books, because 19 books are FREE! I understand that accepting the 3 free books and gifts places me under no obligation to buy anything. I can always return a shipment and cancel at any time. My free books and gifts are mine to keep no matter what I decide.

272 HCN 3070 472 HCN 3070

Name	(PLEASE PRINT)	
Address		Apt. #
City	State/Prov.	Zip/Postal Code

Signature (if under 18, a parent or guardian must sign)

Mail to the **Reader Service:**
IN U.S.A.: P.O. Box 1867, Buffalo, NY 14240-1867
IN CANADA: P.O. Box 609, Fort Erie, Ontario L2A 5X3

* Terms and prices subject to change without notice. Prices do not include applicable taxes. Sales tax applicable in N.Y. Canadian residents will be charged applicable taxes. This offer is limited to one order per household. All orders subject to approval. Credit or debit balances in a customer's account(s) may be offset by any other outstanding balance owed by or to the customer. Please allow 4 to 6 weeks for delivery. Offer available while quantities last. Offer not available to Quebec residents.

WPBPA16R

READERSERVICE.COM

Manage your account online!

- Review your order history
- Manage your payments
- Update your address

*We've designed the
Reader Service website
just for you.*

Enjoy all the features!

- Discover new series available to you, and read excerpts from any series.
- Respond to mailings and special monthly offers.
- Connect with favorite authors at the blog.
- Browse the Bonus Bucks catalog and online-only exculsives.
- Share your feedback.

Visit us at:
ReaderService.com